"Maybe if we kissed we'd realize that it's not that special anymore."

Jessie felt like an idiot for suggesting it. Payson still said nothing, so she stammered, "I-it would prove that all of that is behind us."

"You need to kiss me to prove to yourself...what exactly?" he asked. He shifted in the chair and rolled his shoulders, something he did when he was tense.

"I'm looking at this the way you would—scientifically. We were married. We're not anymore, but we're working together. We're both remembering how it was, and it probably wasn't like we remember anyway. We need to prove to ourselves that there's nothing there."

"The theory that you'd like to test is that if we kiss, we'll discover that what we had was pretty ordinary?"

"Something like that. I'm just trying to be honest here. I know you feel the tension. I've seen those looks and I know what they mean. If we just kiss and get it out of the way, we'll be good to go."

"When would you like to conduct this experiment?"

"What about now?"

Dear Reader,

The first time I visited Arizona as a teen, I fell in love with the desert, cowboys and fry bread (yum!). I fell in love with writing and storytelling even earlier than that and have been a reporter, PR flunky and now a full-fledged romance author. In fact, my reporting led directly to Jessie and Payson's reunion love story.

I was assigned to write a magazine article about a former rodeo trick rider who started a therapeutic horsemanship program. Her amazing dedication sparked an idea that became *The Surgeon and the Cowgirl*.

Of course, I didn't realize how stubborn Cowgirl Jessie and Surgeon Payson would be. After all, they'd fallen in love in high school and were obviously still in love, despite divorce and soul-deep hurts. Getting them to admit that their love had endured *and* that they had changed required the help of a diva pony, endearing kids and meddling family.

Jessie and Payson's happily-ever-after inspired another story. Spencer, Payson's brother, will do anything—even enter into a marriage of convenience to a cowgirl with rodeo dreams—to get back his son in my next book, *The Convenient Cowboy*, coming in August from Harlequin American Romance.

I've loved writing about these strong cowgirls who lasso their men into forever with humor, heart and a sexy wiggle or two.

If you want to know more about my inspirations and musings or drop me a note, check out my website and blog at heidihormel.net, where you also can sign up for my newsletter, or connect with me at facebook.com/authorheidihormel, twitter.com/heidihormel or pinterest.com/hhormel.

Yee-haw,

Heidi Hormel

THE SURGEON AND THE COWGIRL

HEIDI HORMEL

HARLEQUIN® AMERICAN ROMANCE®

ISBN-13: 978-0-373-75573-8

The Surgeon and the Cowgirl

Copyright © 2015 by Heidi Hormel

Printed in U.S.A.

www.Harlequin.com

ABOUT THE AUTHOR

With stints as an innkeeper, radio talk show host and craft store manager, **Heidi Hormel** settled into her true calling as a writer. She spent years as a reporter (covering the story of the rampaging elephants Debbie and Tina) and as a PR flunky (staying calm in the face of Cookiegate) before settling into penning romances with a wink and a wiggle.

A small-town girl from a place that's been called the Snack Food Capital of the World, Heidi has trotted over a good portion of the globe, from Volcano National Park in Hawaii to Loch Ness in Scotland to the depths of Death Valley. She has also spent large chunks of time in Arizona, where she fell in love with the desert and fry bread, and in Great Britain, where she developed an unnatural obsession with jacket potatoes and toasties.

Heidi is on the web at heidihormel.net as well as socially out there at facebook.com/authorheidihormel, twitter.com/heidihormel and pinterest.com/hhormel.

For my patient family, friends and Harlequin author-mentors who have cheered me on and commiserated with me over the past five years and more, this book's for you.

Chapter One

Jessie saw the little boy slip into the corral before anyone else did. *For cripes' sake*, Jessie said silently, adding a litany of choice words as she raced after him, her knee throbbing with every pounding step. The corral was home to two geldings and a mare pacing nervously.

"Alex!" the little boy's mother screamed when the gelding trotted by him. Jessie couldn't waste her time or her breath to tell the silly woman to keep quiet. Instead, she focused on Alex as he stumbled through the uneven dirt, agitating the horses into snorting, then lashing the air with their hooves way too close to Alex's head.

He could have been her son; others had said so when he first came to the program. Her heart clenched every time she heard it. Alex's warm caramel curls were streaked blond from the sun, and his eyes tilted just a little at the corners, like hers.

The horses' hooves pounded faster as she made her way across the dusty corral. She had to get him out. Now.

"Alex, sweetie," Jessie said softly but firmly once she was beside him. She knew her height could be overwhelming for a little guy, so she squatted next to him. Her knee popped and cracked. Years of rodeo trick riding had left her two legacies: enough money to open

Hope's Ride and battered joints. "Come on, Alex. Let's go see Mommy."

"No," the little boy said with a shake of his head.

"I know you want to ride the horses, sweetie, but it's time for you to go home. The horses need a nap," Jessie said.

The scuffling of hooves and the wet snorts increased in pace. Even with her experience, Jessie wouldn't be able to stop them if they got themselves into a full-out panic. She considered just grabbing Alex and running. Problem—she and running had parted ways years ago, exactly when her knee had been torn up to heck and back.

But, then, Alex suddenly took a few unsteady steps and fell. Small for his age from years of surgeries and his disease, he was at Hope's Ride to strengthen his muscles and build his confidence. Jessie scooted forward while he righted himself to sit in the dirt, tears streaking his dusty face. She wanted to pick him up, but she knew that his manly pride-in-the-making had been bruised from his fall. Coddling from her or anyone else would lead to a full-out kicking, screaming fit. The horses paced faster, tossing their heads with agitation.

"You can give Molly her treat if you come with me now," Jessie said, keeping her voice gentle, despite every instinct that told her to get moving. "Molly likes you best, you know. I bet she's hoping right now that you're the one bringing her the apple today." Molly, Jessie's childhood pony, had two speeds—slow and slower— making her a perfect introduction to riding for children who were reluctant to approach the large horses.

"Okay. I like Molly," Alex said. "She gives me kisses." He got up but didn't move. This meant that he was willing to have help. Jessie stood, too, ignoring her protesting knee.

"Great. How about I carry you back to the fence? That would be fun, wouldn't it?" Jessie asked as she leaned down. He reached up.

She heard an increase in the snorts and pounding of hooves as the threesome rushed by. She knew that they'd stampede in seconds. The corral fence was fifteen or twenty feet away. Even if she could run, moving like that would just add to the horses' agitation. With the big animals taking their cues from the humans around them, Jessie saw the disastrous day taking a ninety-degree turn for the worse when Alex's mom crawled between the rails of the fence.

The woman started running, yelling and waving her arms. The idiot, Jessie thought, just as she heard the thunder of hooves coming closer and caught the glimpse of a tall man moving smoothly and surely through the fence.

The horses went into a galloping panic. Jessie stood still to create a patch of calm.

"Mommy," Alex yelled. He wiggled against her side where he clung, drumming his dangling feet hard enough against her thigh that she loosened her grip for a moment. He broke away. She saw the gelding, Dickie, bearing down on them, his hooves huge and his eyes rimmed in white. Jessie reached out—thank God she was close enough to nab Alex. In the same motion, she folded him under her as the gelding raced over them. The large horse instinctively lifted himself to jump over the obstacle in his path. Jessie braced herself for the smack of a hoof, but Dickie had cleared them. She didn't move. She had to protect the boy.

"Jessie, get the hell out of here," said a familiar deep voice from behind her, followed by a strong grip on her forearm lifting her up. She scrambled to curl over and protect the little boy. Payson, her ex-husband, kept his grip on her, while Alex's mother, who'd been pulled to the other side of the fence, was being held in place by program volunteers.

"Alex," she said, working to break free, as panicked as the horses. She had to keep him safe. It was her job. Her responsibility.

"I've got him," Payson said, easily lifting the child with his other hand. He tucked Alex under his arm. Dickie passed by again, but this time he gave them plenty of space, and the other horses were now being calmed by ranch hands.

Taller than her by a hand span, Payson moved quickly as he carried Alex and dragged her behind him, toward Alex's mother, who openly cried. He had them out of the corral before Jessie could catch her breath. He ignored her as he turned to Alex, running his strong, lean surgeon's hands expertly over him. It'd always amazed Jessie that Payson never intimidated children with his height. Could be his controlled calmness made them feel safe. When he was younger, his buttoned-up veneer had screamed prep school, but she'd always loved the dark intensity of his gaze, even when it reminded her of a big bad wolf eying a juicy jackrabbit.

Back in their day, when she'd see that look, she had to fight the urge to rip off her clothes and get him belly to belly in bed. And whenever she'd given in, once those starched and pressed clothes were off, she'd explored every inch of his tautly muscled body, one that always surprised her by being more cowboy than egghead. But that was back when she was young and didn't know the difference between lust and love. A few years of living with Payson had finally taught her the yawning gap between the two.

Alex would be fine with him. Payson's talent for healing children was the only reason he was here. Jessie would suck it up and court him to gain his hospital's stamp of approval for her program. Once she had that, then she'd get a steady stream of patients who would make Hope's Ride a paying operation. Right now, her dream of helping youngsters drained her savings account more and more each month.

Jessie turned away from the man and the memories. She needed to check on the horses and the other children. She also needed a few minutes to give her heart a chance to stop racing and to find a private place to have a cry.

Usually Payson stayed focused when he was working with patients but not today. Not with Jessie limping away from him. She wore her usual jeans and a Western shirt with the sleeves rolled up. Her cowboy boots were battered and broken in. Before the divorce—not now, of course—her casual outfit would get him hot under his suddenly tight collar. Physical closeness and sexual intensity had never been the problems in their marriage. It had been just about everything else, especially her devotion to the rodeo and her horses. He'd been amazed to hear that she'd retired from trick riding and wondered what had happened. It didn't matter, he reminded himself. She wasn't his wife. She wasn't his problem. She'd made that clear when she'd walked out and never looked back.

"Dr. MacCormack, are you sure he's okay? He looks

a little flushed," Alex's mom said, finally getting Payson's attention by touching his arm.

"You're just fine, aren't you, buddy?" Payson asked the little boy standing next to him. "Bring him in tomorrow, so I can check that ligament in his arm. I've been meaning to do that anyway, right?"

He was sure the boy had not been hurt, but with a child like Alex, he couldn't leave anything to chance. Since Alex's birth, Payson had overseen the boy's care, including the multiple surgeries he'd endured in his short life. The geneticists insisted that he was affected by an unnamed syndrome. For Alex, the vague diagnosis meant that he had fragile tendons and ligaments that tore easily and stretched so that his bones became misaligned.

Payson had been annoyed that Karin, Alex's mom, had put him in the riding program, especially one run by his ex-wife. There were too many things that could go wrong. And he should know. He'd seen Jessie with bruises and broken bones. He knew intellectually that the therapy program had little or nothing in common with the trick riding that Jessie loved. Still, his gut insisted that the chances for recovery equaled the chances for injury. Not that his gut mattered. Evidence. Scientific evidence was all that was relevant. Jessie might run on gut and feeling, but not him.

He looked over his shoulder at his ex-wife, who hadn't gone very far before one of the program's volunteers stopped her. She didn't look all that different from when they had married ten years ago—when she'd been nineteen and he twenty—in a ceremony that had given his Chanel-wearing mother heart palpitations.

Jessie's blond-streaked hair was still long enough to

pull through the back opening of her ball cap and trail down her back. She might have been a native Arizonan, but she only wore a Stetson when she was riding in the rodeo parade. He didn't need to be close to know that her eyes remained the smoky green of sagebrush. She might be tall and thin, but muscles, earned every day by riding, cleaning stalls and moving hay bales, gave her a shape that filled out her jeans and her pearl-buttoned shirt.

Not that those curves affected him anymore. Obviously. When he had the time and interest to start dating, he'd choose a woman who moved in the same circles as his family, a woman who wore stilettos and never dusty, scarred boots. He might not be close to his parents, the way Jessie was with hers, but finding an "appropriate" woman might help him find common ground with his mother and father.

"Molly," Alex said. "I want to give Molly her apple. Miss Jessie promised."

Payson could hear the rising hysteria in Alex's voice. Why wasn't the boy's mother calming him? Instead, Karin fluttered around and looked at Payson to intervene.

"Next time, Alex," Jessie said as she neared them. "Molly understands that you need to go home today. How about you wave goodbye?"

"No," Alex said and shook his head. "I want to give Molly her apple."

With more fluttering from Karin, Alex's face got redder. Payson picked up the boy, thinking briefly that he could've had a child around Alex's age. His and Jessie's child. "Which one?" he asked shortly.

Jessie didn't say a word but moved off slowly. He followed, refusing to notice how her Wrangler jeans outlined the shift and roll of her muscles. Alex chattered and Payson nodded absently during the mercifully short walk.

"Wave goodbye, Alex," Jessie said. The little boy waved his arm and a fat Shetland pony that looked vaguely familiar raised her head and gave a long friendly whinny on cue, followed by a bouncing jog to the fence.

Alex wanted more, though, and wiggled and squirmed until Payson finally put him on his own feet. The boy, holding tight to Payson's hand, walked to where the pony had its nose forced between the slats of the fence.

"She wants to give me a kiss," Alex explained as they neared. The boy put his cheek to the pony's lips, and Molly nibbled gently, making the boy squeal in delight. Payson braced himself for the animal to bite Alex or lash out with a hoof. Instead, the pony looked as though she was smiling as she pulled away and shook her mane into place. Her head came back through the fence and Alex tugged on Payson's arm. "She wants to kiss you now."

"It's time to go," Payson said.

"No. Molly wants to kiss you."

"Yes, Payson," Jessie said, laughter clear in her voice. "Molly likes giving kisses."

"No. She only likes to kiss little boys, and I'm not a little boy," he answered. No way was he letting that pony near him with its mouth or any other body part. Molly's lips smacked together, and Alex tugged on him again. "Fine. I'll let her give me a kiss if Miss Jessie gives me a kiss, too."

He knew it was a challenge. One he was sure that Jessie would decline. Instead, she snapped, "No problem." Her surprisingly soft lips curled into an evil grin.

Payson leaned over so the pony could touch her lips

to his cheek. The smell of oats and molasses wafted over him as the little animal chuffed a breath across his face. He pulled back quickly. Jessie grinned. He reached up his hand to check his face. Slimy pony slobber. He strode forward before Jessie could move and wiped his cheek on hers. She laughed, and he covered her mouth with his to wipe that smirk off her face. Their lips met, and hers parted and softened. *Damn.* His hand moved down her back, and he pulled her close.

"Dr. Mac, Dr. Mac, I want to go now."

Saved by the kid, Payson thought. No way he resented that. He and Jessie were over long ago. Having his heart ripped out once was more than enough. "Sure, Alex. Let's go." He easily swung the boy up into his arms and carried him to his mother's car.

He knew what—if he went with his knee-jerk reaction—he'd tell the hospital administration about the program: therapy riding posed an imminent danger to patients. He'd seen a youngster miss being trampled by inches. He would *not* talk about what had happened to his brain when he saw Jessie go into that corral. Time had stopped. That usually only happened during surgery, when everything went away except the small field of skin exposed by draped hospital fabric. When the seconds stretched out, making each of his movements deliberate and slow. Often after surgery, he was surprised by the amount of time that had passed.

"He's going to be okay, right?" Jessie asked as they watched the boy and his mom drive away.

"Yes," he said tightly, not willing to argue with her about safety right now. "What about you? What's up with your knee?"

"Nothing." She shifted, and the silence stretched between them, tense and heated. "I want to invite you to come back another day. Alex is doing really well out here. In fact, so well that he's starting to misbehave because he has the strength and confidence."

Jessie's gaze didn't waver as she looked at him. *Double damn.* It was as hard saying no to her as to Alex, which was exactly why he'd been reluctant to evaluate this program. On the other hand, when the administration "asked" a doctor to do something, it was never good for his career to refuse. Now that he was involved, he needed to step back and act like the scientist he was. Could he formulate any conclusions after only one visit? He really hadn't had a chance to assess the program before Alex's great escape. Spending more time with Jessie and her program was strictly in the interest of research.

"My schedule is full for the next week," he said in his professional voice. "Call me at the hospital and talk with my office manager. Maybe she can find time in two or three weeks."

Payson watched Jessie's face change from resolute to angry. "Two or three weeks? This is important, Payson."

"I know, but so are my patients. I have operations back-to-back, and then clinic and—"

"You don't have to tell me. I know."

He could see she was both upset and disappointed. "Before I go, I want to check that knee."

"I'm fine."

"Who's the doctor here?" It was a familiar argument and one that could almost make him smile. They had teased each other often like that early in their marriage, until those teasing comments had become angry barbs. He stepped toward her, and she didn't back up. He could smell Jessie's seductive scent, a mix of hay, desert mesquite and Ivory soap. He'd discovered on their third or fourth date that just a brief whiff aroused him. If he'd thought the kiss had gotten him hot, it was nothing compared to her fragrance. He looked at her and saw a flush on her face that wasn't from the sun.

He made himself step back. They were divorced. "You should use ice followed by heat. Take a double dose of ibuprofen today and tomorrow morning and that should keep the swelling down and help with the pain."

"Thanks, Doc," she said. "I'll call the office."

"You do that. I've got to go."

She put her hand on his arm to stop him from turning. "He really is a great kid, Payson. He's been doing so well. At first he was weak and scared, but now he's walking more often and his balance is thirty percent improved. The therapy works."

"I said I'd come back," he answered, not wanting to argue with her, rail at her that he'd also seen Alex almost get trampled to death. He'd learned a few things in their years apart, including how to keep his temper in check. What he hadn't learned was how to erase the memory of her curled against him when they were alone and in their big old-fashioned sleigh bed—the bed he still slept in. There were nights when the dreams were so real he'd wake up and reach for her. When he felt the coolness of the empty sheets, he wanted to cry or punch the wall.

He needed to sell that bed.

Chapter Two

Jessie glared at Payson, who was sitting across from her three weeks after his disastrous visit in his version of cowboy casual—a pressed and starched shirt tucked into equally stiff, dark denims. It was wrong to iron jeans, as she had told him more than once, and it was wrong for her to think he looked sexy.

They were in her small office that was crammed into the corner of one of the barns. Usually the scents of hay and horse kept her calm and focused. Not today. Three years divorced, and he could still make her mad enough to see red. What did she tell the kids to do when they were angry? Walk away. Well, she didn't have a choice about that this time. Payson had just announced that if she wanted the hospital to endorse her program, then he was sticking around.

"Your neck is red and not from the sun," he said softly, his mouth curling a little as his coffee-colored eyes gleamed with a wry humor. "Are you upset?"

She waited for him to laugh. One snort. One chortle and she was taking him down. She regularly wrestled with a half ton of horse. "I am surprised. A barn is the last place I expected you to want to hang out," she said.

"Times change."

"You mean it's snowing in hell."

"I would think you'd watch your language with all of these children around."

She didn't want to fight with him, but he definitely knew which buttons to push. "Do you have any ideas on how you would like to carry out your observations?"

"You mean besides stand and watch?" he asked and grinned.

She worked not to smile back at that smart-ass answer. Those sorts of comments had gotten him into trouble on a regular basis when they were younger. Of course, there were times when the verbal battle that followed such remarks would lead directly to a horizontal two-step, but she was not going there today…or any other day, she told her racing heart. She calmly said, "We're using the indoor ring. That would probably be the best place to start."

Payson had told her that he would observe again today. After that, he and the team from the hospital would be at the ranch nearly full-time to see how the program aligned with medical standards. Jessie had never expected that the hospital would take such a hands-on approach, but if she wanted to keep Hope's Ride operating, she had to accept the invasion. She'd try to cooperate. She really would. It was just tough with Payson as the one coordinating the study by the hospital.

He stood and waited. She got up and limped off through the barn. It had been weeks since her tussle with Alex and the horse, but her knee refused to stop aching. Being short-handed at the ranch hadn't helped her condition. She'd been doing more than usual, and going to the doctor was out of the question. Until Hope's Ride made money, Jessie had only the most basic insurance.

Payson followed her, making her even more self-conscious about her gait. In the past, when he'd walked behind her, he'd said it was so he could enjoy how she filled out a pair of jeans. She doubted that was what he felt right now.

"Here's the indoor ring," Jessie said. She would pretend he was a donor who was thinking about supporting Hope's Ride. That would give her the right attitude. "The afternoon sessions are for the younger children who aren't in school yet."

He looked at his watch. "I have a consultation at three, so that gives us an hour."

Jessie almost made a snarky comment. *Paste on a smile and be polite*, she firmly told herself. She could do that for the next hour. She could do that for however long it was going to take to save Hope's Ride.

She explained briefly what the volunteers were doing and each child's therapy plan. Payson asked questions, but his gaze was intent on the children. They stood side by side for a few moments. She could smell the tartness of the starch from his shirt and clearly remembered what that innocent-looking cotton hid. She would not think about how that scent had invaded her senses when Alex made them kiss.

She refused to remember how he had touched her in their big comfortable bed—a whimsical monstrosity that Payson had bought for her because she'd refused to have a diamond ring. During the divorce, she'd told him nastily that she didn't want anything from their marriage, especially that "stupid" bed. Less than a year later, a stumble by Candy Cane, her Appaloosa, had changed her life as much as marrying Payson at nineteen had. While her damaged knee functioned pretty well, it wasn't 100 percent and never would be. She'd had to retire from the rodeo.

After a month of sitting at her folks' house in Tucson and feeling sorry for herself, her parents placed a firm, but kindly, foot on her butt, encouraging her to open Hope's Ride. The program had been in her someday plans after seeing riding therapy in action at a farm in Ohio. So, after paying her medical bills, she'd used a chunk of her savings along with a little bit of help from her parents and their friends in the rodeo "family" to get started.

Now, every month had become a balancing act of draining her savings as she tried to put off creditors until the payments came in. The problem was that the payments weren't covering all of the expenses now, and her savings were nearly gone.

"Each of the volunteers and paid staff go through extensive training," she told Payson. "The mounts have all been donated. We test each one before any child is allowed on. You can see that each rider has a helmet and helpers. It's very safe. The movement of the horse forces them to—"

"What conditions do you treat?" he asked, interrupting her.

He was a "donor" she reminded herself, and explained the current program and her hopes for expansion. After another five minutes of observation, he suggested that they move on. She took him to the outdoor facilities and to a small room where the children and their caregivers regularly met to speak with the two other therapeutic riding instructors, both of whom were certified. She had help from a couple of part-timers to care for the stock and everyone else volunteered their time and expertise to help the children. She took him into the horse barn. It was empty except for a cat and flies that buzzed lazily in the air.

"The older riders are expected to help care for the horses," Jessie said.

"Free labor, huh?"

"No, Payson, the children, especially the teens, need that kind of responsibility. They don't have a lot of confidence in their own abilities. Caring for the horses shows them that they have a lot more going on than they think."

"Plus a rider always takes care of her own horse," he said, nodding a little as he repeated the words she'd told him often enough.

"Yep. There's that, too. It's also a chance for the kids to really bond with the horses. It's an important part of the therapy."

The tour was over, and they were standing in the aisle of the barn. Even with the sun streaming in through the stalls, it was dim, the concrete floor keeping the space cool. Jessie couldn't see Payson's expression, but his stance was taut. She shifted to give her knee a rest.

He took her arm and said, "That's it. You're going to let me look at that knee."

She started to pull away but his fingers tightened. Her arm tingled where he touched her skin. "It's fine, Payson."

"It is not fine. You were limping the last time I was here, and you're still limping."

"I have an appointment for next week."

"No, you don't. You're lying. You turned your head," he said.

Darn it. How could she have forgotten that he knew her better than anyone else?

"You're a kid doctor. I'm an adult," she said.

"A knee is a knee. Do we have to go through this again? I wanted to look at it the last time I was here."

"I said no then, too. You don't owe me anything, Payson."

"Who said anything about owing you?" he asked. "I'm trying to fulfill my duty as a physician."

PAYSON GRITTED HIS TEETH. Why did Jessie have to make things so hard? She had this idea that if she didn't do things herself, people would never respect her. So, here they were glaring at each other. The way she favored her leg, it must be excruciating.

When they'd been married, she'd often ridden with something pulled or strained. Jessie was used to being hurt and not showing it. He remembered her eyes shining with tears more than once and her fighting to keep them from spilling down her cheeks. The code of the rodeo, she'd told him. "You don't let people see you cry no matter how much you hurt." It was all about respect. That was what was driving her to limp around on a knee that needed rest and attention.

He glanced at his watch. He was already late for his consult, and he tried to ignore the hitch in his stomach from the same tug of war that had strained their marriage: patients or Jessie. With more heat than he intended, he said, "You need to have that checked out."

"I will if it doesn't get any better."

He followed her from the barn, his concern as a physician fighting with his intense arousal as he watched her tall, lithe body shift under her just-tight-enough clothing. In the old days, even when he'd been exhausted during his surgical residency, following her around like this would have made him hot enough to not care about schedules or exams. He would have dragged her into one of the stalls and…

Why would he remember any of their marriage fondly? Sure, it had been amazing when their problems could be solved by a little time together in bed. When they had to deal with the real problems, grown-up problems, everything fell apart.

"I'll see you tomorrow at ten. I'll be done with rounds by then," he said as he got into his Range Rover.

"I'll have the releases you requested ready and the therapy plans, too. 'Bye," she said and turned without another word.

He jammed the SUV into Drive and gravel spit from his tires.

As HELEN, HIS office manager, laid out the medication and instruments he requested, she said, "A doctor who makes house calls? Wait till I tell your other patients, they'll be lining up."

"Thank you," Payson said, giving her an aggravated look.

"Oooh, the Dr. Mac evil eye. I'm so scared," she said and laughed. "Based on what's being said in the halls, I'm guessing this has to do with Jessie?" Her voice had gone from joking to aggravated.

"The grapevine is pretty quick," Payson said. He was irked that he and Jessie were being discussed, but it was a hospital. There was no way to stop the rumors. He needed to stay focused on his final goal: becoming director of pediatrics. It had been made clear to him that moving up at the hospital now depended on the success of the program. He and his team were expected to bring Hope's Ride into compliance with the hospital's goals and policies.

"It's a practical thing," he explained to Helen. "She's got to be at a hundred percent if I want to get her program integrated with ours." He saw Helen start to open her mouth and he looked at her from beneath slightly lowered brows. That one gesture had been known to quiet children in a full tantrum. "She injured her knee saving Alex Suarez. Even you have to agree that examining her is the least I can do as a doctor. I'm sure she doesn't have very good insurance. Plus, I need to speak with her about the hospital's requirements."

"I would guess that there are hundreds of doctors in the greater Phoenix area who would treat her," Helen said. She straightened the stacks of paper on his desk, her mouth tight and disapproving. Payson imagined it was how a mother would look when her child had acted up. His own mother had always let the nanny or school take care of it when Payson or his brother misbehaved.

"I've got to finish up," Helen said. "My son has a lacrosse game this afternoon."

When she left, Payson focused on the consult he'd just had and the endless paperwork for his other patients. He knew that, as director of pediatrics, most of his day would be filled with paperwork like this. That was the downside. As he'd told Helen again and again, he could be more effective in helping care for children as director. What he would never admit was that by becoming an administrator and sacrificing what he really loved— performing surgery—he might finally make up for not being able to save the one small life that had mattered more to him than any other.

JESSIE SAT STIFFLY in her office chair as Payson pressed and poked her knee. She'd only agreed to let him check the joint after he'd refused to continue the evaluation of Hope's Ride until she let him examine her. She wanted to squirm away but felt stupid because he didn't seem affected by nearly lying in her lap as he prodded the knee. Her skin prickled with awareness and she ground her teeth against the moan...of pain. Definitely pain.

"When are you going to have this knee replaced?" he asked as he sat back on his heels.

She relaxed a little. "I'm not. At least, not until I'm ninety."

"You're dreaming. I'm sure the surgeon told you that this reconstruction was temporary at best. That knee will need to be replaced. Probably sooner rather than later," Payson said as he put away his instruments and kept his back to her.

"It works fine for what I do now. I just tweaked it helping Alex. Now, can we get started? The kids are waiting for us," she said. She went to the door, trying hard not to limp.

Payson followed her outdoors, where children were preparing to mount up. The pony, Molly, trotted around the ring, herding stragglers toward the volunteers and caregivers. The hospital observers stood clear of all the commotion. It took a good fifteen minutes to get the children settled and the therapy started. Even so, there were stops for tears and more than one potty break.

"Is this how the program usually operates? I don't remember observing this sort of chaos previously," Payson asked.

"More or less. We're careful to not push the children too hard. They are fairly new to riding. We don't want to make them hate it before they discover the joy," Jessie said.

"There definitely needs to be more structure," he said as he made a notation.

"I understand why you may think that, but I am trained, you know. I've found that—"

"I understand that you took, what, a one-year course?" Payson asked without looking up.

He made it sound as if she didn't know what she was doing, just like when they'd been married.

He went on as he closed his notebook and looked her in the eye. "I wanted to let you know that I had a meeting this morning before I came out here. There are additional concerns about the program and the affiliation."

"You mean concerns that you brought up. I should have known there was no way you would give the program a fair evaluation."

"I'm not any more thrilled about this situation than you are. It has been made completely clear to me that to become director of pediatrics, I've got to work with you to get this program ready for an affiliation with the hospital."

"What the hell does that mean?"

"Jessie, language."

"I only swear when you're around."

"I doubt that," he said and looked out over the ring. The youngsters rode slowly with big grins on their faces. "I gave a brief report this morning to the committee, and they decided that their involvement needs to be more extensive."

"Than what? You're here with who knows how many others. I lost count," Jessie said.

"I'm going to bottom-line it. The hospital will be overseeing the program while all of the departments do their evaluations and make their recommendations for changes and upgrades to increase efficiency and effectiveness."

"Payson, please follow me," Jessie said tightly. She could not have this conversation anywhere near the children because she was going to be yelling and possibly committing murder. When they were fifty feet from the corral, she turned to him. "This is my program. I know I contacted you, but just to ask who I should talk to at the hospital. I never asked for you to take over. You always have to be the one in control, don't you? You can't let me do this on my own. It's just like when we were married. You were always trying to improve things—like telling me I should go to college and diagramming the most economical way to do laundry."

"Jessie, if I want to be named the director I've got to make this program work for the hospital. It'll be good for you, too. There are a number of departments that are chomping at the bit—pardon the pun—to use your program. It doesn't hurt that, according to the public relations guy, Hope's Ride will make the hospital look 'progressive and forward thinking.'"

"So the children don't matter? It's all about image and your promotion? I'm the one in charge here. It's my program," she said, hoping she sounded stronger than she felt. Had she hoped he'd come back for her? Not to climb up the hospital rungs?

"Jessie, if you don't work with me and the others, the hospital will cut off any association. I know a few doctors have given the program a try. They will take away their patients and no one else will refer children to you. It won't take long for word to get around that there must be something wrong since Desert Valley Hospital won't refer anyone."

If she wanted her program to continue, she had to give

in. If she were a millionaire, like the members of the hospital's board, she could tell them to take a flying leap.

"By the way, I did convince the hospital to give you a stipend out of my budget while I run the program."

"Excuse me. Back up. You're going to be doing what?"

"I'll be in charge of Hope's Ride while the hospital staff is here."

"You've got to be kidding me. You're going to be my boss?"

Chapter Three

"I won't exactly be your boss," Payson said.

"You're paying me. You're telling me what to do. Seems like that's *exactly* what a boss does," Jessie fired back.

He was wary because when she was upset, she sometimes acted before she thought. "If you want the hospital to list you as an endorsed program, you're going to have to accept this condition for now."

"Fine. I'm sure you're happy, Dr. Control Freak."

"If I were your boss, comments like that would get you fired," he said, only half-joking.

"Good thing that you're not 'exactly' my boss then."

"Maybe setting some ground rules would help. I'll give you a written list of the protocols that will need to be followed. That's not my choice. It's the hospital's rules." He saw her lips go from full to thin and waited for the explosion.

"I understand," she finally said, not looking any less annoyed but sounding…resigned.

"Great. That's a start," he said.

Her capitulation didn't make him feel like they were on better footing. He didn't want her program to fail. He'd never wished that anything bad would happen to

Jessie—at least, not anymore. The first few months after the divorce, he might have hoped that she'd have to ride rodeo in Siberia.

They talked for a few more minutes. By the end of the conversation, Payson thought there was a good chance that the two of them could work together with minimal conflict. He hoped so, because his future had been firmly tied to Jessie's by the hospital. "Tomorrow, we'll plan for the team from physical therapy to observe. They talked about wanting to stay for two weeks, then they'll make recommendations. At that point, we'll discuss how to assess the success of those improvements."

"Improvements? Yeah, I can already see the improvements, like making sure that you don't let the kids actually near the horses, or filling out useless forms because you want to have *documentation*."

"Jessie, there are certain standards that must be met, but I'm sure we can find compromises. That's why we're here—to determine the best way to proceed and benefit both of us," Payson said, wondering if that sounded as pompous as it did in his head.

"Save the bullsh—you know what. I know there's no use arguing with you. I'll save it for the therapists. I have a feeling they'll be more reasonable anyway," she said and went on before he could protest. "I'd like to set up an orientation for all of your staff. I know they know their jobs but most won't have worked around horses. Even my volunteers who are horse people have to go through orientation. It keeps everyone safe. Why don't you join the first group—that'll let everyone know how important it is."

Was she suggesting that he wasn't taking the collaboration seriously? "Absolutely," he said. "Administration 101—lead by example."

"Yeah, I guess," she said, looking at him oddly.

In the spirit of working together, he didn't comment. He didn't have the time anyway. They were largely silent as they headed to his Range Rover, when Jessie said tentatively, "Alex's next therapy session might be a good chance for you to observe."

He paused and wondered if this was a Jessie-style olive branch. "I'll have to check my schedule."

"Great. See you at orientation," she said.

"See you then," he said. They stood by his SUV. Jessie scuffed the dirt with her boot. Should he shake her hand? No. Even that small contact would stay with him the rest of the day, making him aware that his physical desire for her—and that's all it was, he assured himself—hadn't gotten the memo about the divorce and the three years apart. He did wave as he bumped down the lane.

"EVERYTHING'S FINE, MAMA," Jessie said patiently into her cell. "The hospital is really happy with the program. It won't take long for them to give me the okay."

"If you need money, you let Daddy and me know," her mother said.

Jessie would only accept more money if the horses were going hungry. Her parents and everyone else had already helped her so much—she couldn't ask them for anything more. "I'm good, Mama."

"Are you sure? I know it's gotta be tough working with Payson. I know how badly he hurt you," her mother said, a *tsk* in her voice. Her mother had been equally disappointed with Jessie and Payson when the marriage had ended.

Jessie didn't want to talk about what had happened. She'd let go of the sadness and the resentment—she'd been sure—or she'd never have called Payson about Hope's Ride. Since he'd shown up, she'd been replaying their marriage, both good and bad. It all got on her last nerve. "Mama, Payson and I are doing fine. This is about Hope's Ride and him moving up at the hospital. It's just business."

"Mm-hmm," her mother said. "I'm not too partial to those TV advice doctors, but you know they're always asking people, 'How will that work for you?' So, how do you think that's going to work?"

"I told you, it's business."

"That's what you said. But, really, darlin', how can it ever be strictly business between the two of you?"

"We're divorced, Mama. That's all there is."

"You know how I feel about that divorce," her mama said, "but that horse left the barn years ago. Do you think this is your chance to settle things between you? You know, talk about—"

"We are *not* talking about the past. That's over. This is about Hope's Ride."

"Is it in the past? Why did you call Payson in the first place?"

Jessie knew this answer. "Because he works at the best pediatric hospital in the valley."

"Mmm-hmm. What about that teaching hospital that was looking for programs that use alternative therapies? I remember Daddy tellin' you about it. He saw it on the news."

"Desert Valley is better," Jessie said stubbornly.

"Darlin', that may be true, too, but that's not why you called Payson."

"It's the only reason, Mama. Hope's Ride needs to be endorsed by and affiliated with only the best hospital. Plus a lot of my kids have doctors there."

"And at every other hospital in the valley. You are a very smart girl. Even you should be able to figure out why you called on Payson when you were in trouble."

"It's business, Mama," Jessie said, and even she could hear the desperation in her voice. Business was the only reason. She was over Payson. She was the one who'd filed for the divorce, for goodness' sake. "Having Desert Valley's stamp of approval will give me a cushion and let me expand in a few years, branch out to help more children."

"Any hospital could have given you that cushion."

"Mama, I have to go. I have orientation for the hospital staff today, and then we've got a full day of therapy," Jessie broke in.

Her mother gave a gusty sigh. "Baby girl, you know I love you no matter what. But I swear you and Payson need your heads knocked together. Just business. Not likely. Now, you go and get to work."

It was hard to get her mother's voice out of her thoughts. In the dark days when Jessie had been considering divorce, Mama had counseled against it. Instead, she said that Jessie and Payson needed to talk and maybe see a professional. Jessie had tried to follow that advice, but it didn't help that when they could actually find time to talk, one of them was always tired and distracted. Their discussions quickly broke down into hurtful fights.

Then Jessie stopped asking her mama for advice and went to visit a divorce lawyer. She had just wanted the pain to end. Perhaps now she could admit that, as she signed her name to the papers, Jessie had known that she and Payson still had unfinished business.

"I THINK THAT went well," Jessie said to Payson as they ended the orientation later in the day. "Even you seemed comfortable around the horses."

"Why are you so surprised? It wasn't like it was the first time I was ever around a horse," he said, giving her a lowered-brow look that was supposed to intimidate her.

"Dr. Mac." Alex's little-boy voice carried easily from where he was getting out of his mother's car and into his wheelchair, which was a sure sign that Alex was having a bad day. "Dr. Mac. You came to see me ride." He bounced in his seat and a grin stretched across his face. His brush with near disaster hadn't dampened his enthusiasm for the horses.

"Sure thing, buddy," Payson said.

Jessie was surprised. He'd told her that he was leaving right after the orientation session because he had a stack of paperwork back at the hospital. She'd been relieved. Without him around, she didn't have to think of the interrupted conversations that she knew they needed to continue. Even in the face of Alex's excitement, a part of her wanted to tell Payson to go—the part that recalled vividly every caress they had ever shared and the part that still got disconcertingly hot and bothered when their arms accidentally brushed or he stood near enough for her to catch the fresh scent of his shaving cream. She said nothing.

"I get to feed Molly her apple today. Miss Jessie promised. 'Member I didn't get to before when you were here and then Mommy wouldn't let me come and now Mommy said this is the last time I'm coming to see Molly, so I gotta give her the apple."

"Your last time?" Payson asked quietly.

Alex pulled on Payson's arm to get him to lean closer

and whispered in a voice that still carried to Jessie. "Mommy said that I couldn't come anymore 'cause they said that there wasn't no more money for riding."

Jessie looked at the little boy's mother and saw her eyes swimming in tears. "Come on, Alex," Jessie said, getting behind his wheelchair. "We've been waiting for you. You ready to ride?"

"Yep," Alex said.

"Are you sure? You got your boots?"

He stretched out a foot. "Yep," he said. This was a game that he and Jessie sometimes played.

"What about jeans? You got your riding jeans on?"

"Yep. Mommy forgot to wash them, but they don't stink too bad."

Jessie leaned over and took a deep sniff. "I don't know. You smell like...road apples," she said with a grin.

"Miss Jessie, what's that? Is that the kind of apple that Molly likes?" Alex asked.

Jessie hesitated, looking back at Payson to see if he'd heard the exchange. He was in deep conversation with Alex's mother. It didn't really matter if he'd heard, she told herself, because Payson wouldn't remember her teasing him about road apples and how it had led to their first date. She was the only one who kept being blindsided by memories of their time together.

Jessie couldn't stop her smile as she explained to Alex that "road apples" was a different way to say horse poop.

He giggled. "Horse doody don't look like apples."

"I guess to whoever made that up, it did," she said. "Time to get riding." She could see his brain continuing to work on the mystery. As she helped Alex onto his mount, she wondered if this would be his last time. Maybe not. Kids often said things that weren't true because they didn't understand what the adults around them were really saying. She tried not to play favorites, but there was something about Alex that tugged at her heart. She couldn't view him as just another patient. How did Payson do this on a regular basis? How did he work with these children and not get his heart ripped out when he couldn't help them or, heaven forbid, they died?

PAYSON WATCHED ALEX find his body's center as Jessie placed him on a small horse for his therapy session. He was beaming. Obviously, sitting on a horse was better than anything that even Santa could've brought him. Payson had spoken with Karin about Alex's comments and discovered the foundation that had been covering the cost of the therapy had to make some tough decisions about what they would fund. Alex and his riding hadn't made the cut.

While Payson may not have been completely convinced of riding's therapeutic outcomes, he could see that there was a psychological benefit in Alex's case. Recently, the little boy had been more positive about his limitations and even more willing to do his conventional therapy. Payson needed actual research before formally agreeing that Hope's Ride made a difference for patients' physical recovery and progress, but in some very specific cases, he could see that the therapy did influence outlook and attitude. The question was whether that improvement made the program worthy of affiliation with a hospital like Desert Valley. If it did, money situations such as Alex's would likely go away.

"Let me give the foundation a call," Payson had finally told Karin as tears streaked down her face. "I'm not promising anything, but maybe I can give them the assurance they need."

"Dr. MacCormack, if you call them, I know they won't say no."

"I don't know about that, but I'll certainly see what I can do," he said, and then asked her questions about Alex's recent regression to the wheelchair. He hadn't seen anything on the X-rays after the boy's fall and nearly getting run over by the horse, but Payson worried there was something that had not shown up immediately. Karin explained that Alex had insisted on the chair because he wanted to save all of his strength for the riding and for feeding Molly. Payson had to smile at Alex's determination to figure out how to work around his illness with as little fuss as possible. Once again, he had to admit that his patient's improved attitude could be attributed to Hope's Ride.

When the session ended, Alex broke into a song that he'd made up on the spot about feeding Molly her apples and getting pony kisses. Payson went to him, while Karin stayed in the arena talking with one of the therapists and another mother.

"Dr. Mac," Alex said. "Are you going to kiss Miss Jessie again?"

"Not this time. And no kisses from Molly, either," he said, hoping that would quiet the boy. He was pretty sure he heard Jessie chuckle.

At the fence, the pony jammed her head between the rails, her lips smacking in anticipation of the apple in Alex's hand. The adults stood a few steps away as Alex fed the pony and talked with her. He told her that he wouldn't be back, but that she shouldn't be sad. "There are other little boys and girls who will give you apples,"

Alex told her, his voice quavering just a little. "Mommy said that someday we'll come out to visit but that might not be for a little while."

Payson had learned not to react to emotion from his patients and their parents. With Alex, he felt his heart wrench with every tear. He desperately wanted to tell his young patient that everything would be fine and that he'd be coming to Hope's Ride as usual. But Payson shouldn't make that promise. If he were director of pediatrics, then he would have leverage to get a "yes" to this and a lot of other options for his patients.

"Don't worry, Alex," he said, squatting beside the boy. "Mommy and I are working to see to it that you'll be back soon. You can work hard on your therapy at the hospital, and I bet you'll do even better the next time you're here."

"Are you sure?" Alex asked.

"Yep. No need for you to worry," Payson said, avoiding looking at Jessie. He also didn't think about the fact that he might just be lying to the boy, and what would happen if he couldn't convince the foundation to pay for the treatment. "Do you think Molly's done with her apple? Your mommy's waiting for you."

"See you, Molly," Alex said, and patted the pony. His smile reached ear to ear. "'Bye, Miss Jessie." He raised his arms for a hug. Payson saw her eyes close as she lifted the boy off the ground and squeezed him tight. When she put him down, Payson was stunned by the pain on her face.

As Alex made his way toward his mother, Payson stepped up to Jessie. "The foundation that helps pay for Alex's therapy is withholding funds, according to Karin. I'll give them a call. I'm sure that something can be worked out."

Turning from him, Jessie said, "He's not the first child who's had to stop coming. Unfortunately, I'm sure he won't be the last. That's why Desert Valley is so important. More places would help out if the hospital gave us its Good Doctoring Seal of Approval."

"I'm making the call to the foundation, Jessie." His time at Hope's Ride had totally messed with his schedule and now his brain was sorting through what he would face when he finally got back to his office. Helen had left six messages and sent him ten texts. The last said, Get your @ss in here.

"You'll make the call today. You won't forgot once you get back to the hospital," Jessie said when she caught him at his vehicle.

"I said I'd do it," he snapped, a little tired of her acting as if he was the bad guy around here.

"Make sure that you do."

"What's that supposed to mean?"

"That you don't believe in this program, and you're just here so that you can get some meaningless title," she said.

"Meaningless? It will mean control over how the children at this hospital are treated. It will mean being able to help more children, being able to offer newer, more effective treatments. And, to do it, I've been scaling back on surgery, which I—" He shook his head before going on. "I've taken on more administrative roles at the hospital. Your program…has changed my plan."

"Of course. Can't mess with the great doctor's plans. Pushing papers is much more important than actually helping the kids."

What the hell? Didn't she understand what it had been like for him to have to say no to children and their parents as he'd started to make the transition to administration? "I was told that this was a 'good trial' to see how I would do as a director because I'll be more or less coordinating the different staffs coming out to the program. If I get this right, I'll have control over all care in pediatrics."

"Now we get to the meat of it. You want to be in control, like always. Haven't you learned anything? These are children, not science experiments."

"I won't apologize for looking for empirical evidence that your program and therapies make a difference. And I'm sure as hell not going to apologize for being a scientist."

"Exactly how are you going to measure happiness, huh?" Jessie said.

"By how well the children are doing on their physical tests and evaluations. The hospital can't base treatments on unicorns and rainbows. There has to be hard data. Do you think that I can tell parents that this is a treatment that will make their child smile? We don't know if it will help him walk again, but isn't it more important that he's smiling? Yes, that's exactly what parents want to hear from their doctor." She was really starting to tick him off.

"You told me that medicine is as much an art as a science. When did you change your mind about that?"

Of all of the things that she would remember from his time as a student, why was that it? He'd thought that way early in his studies, when he'd been full of himself. "I was wrong. It's only about science. I've got to go. We can have this discussion another day when I have data to show you."

"I'll hold you to that and I'll expect an apology when

you find out that I'm right. That the smiles are just as important as the positive MRIs."

"It's a bet."

Chapter Four

Two weeks into the "collaboration" with Desert Valley, Jessie wanted to give everyone the boot, from Payson to his team of experts—experts at being a pain in Jessie's backside. She should have known that the orientation had gone too smoothly to be true. So far, the physical therapists had insisted that they needed another two weeks of observations, and the occupational therapists were still determining how they would "implement the use of adaptive devices." The hospital's risk-management adviser had had the vapors when he'd seen the horses and the carts that they used for the children who couldn't walk. The man had actually had to sit down when the dogs and assorted barn cats rubbed against his pressed khakis.

Of course, the bank called and asked when they could expect the next payment on the line of credit that she'd taken out to buy supplies. Jessie was only a few days past due, but the bank didn't care. She owed. She had to pay. This would have been simple enough if the money hadn't been coming in at a trickle and going out like a fire hose. Jessie had also hoped to borrow a little more money until things turned around. The bank had said clearly and with no hesitation: *No.*

She'd tried talking with each of the team leaders from the hospital with the goal of getting a commitment to end the observation ASAP and get the hospital's endorsement within weeks instead of months. With the hospital on board, Jessie was sure she could go back to the bank to get more credit, which would allow her to take care of her $10,000 balloon payment. Each hospital staffer had succinctly laid out a timeline and emphasized that there was no way to cut one observation or one data collection. Hope's Ride was something totally new to them. They had to be completely sure of its validity and safety. There were no shortcuts.

"What evil idea are you hatching?" Payson asked. They were sitting in the arena watching the children ride, including the recently reinstated Alex.

"No evil idea," she said absently. Could she ask the hospital's therapists to do chores? Like clean the stables? That would mean fewer hours for her paid staff. She hated to cut their wages, but the situation was dire.

"If it involves road apples, it's evil."

Jessie startled herself with her own laughter. "It wasn't my fault you were a city boy and didn't know that road apples had nothing to do with trees."

"My mother had the cook go to six grocery stores looking for them. You told me they were an ancient Native American 'growth enhancer.' And I heard you telling Alex about them. Still teasing us city kids, huh?"

Jessie couldn't keep from grinning. She and Payson had known each other since high school, when more often than not they'd needled each other. "You got me back."

"I did?"

"Sure. In biology lab, you convinced me that, according to my blood type, there was no way that my mama and daddy were my parents. Mrs. Lakewood gave me detention for yelling 'You're a damned liar' at you."

"That doesn't count. You punched me after school. I fell and got a bloody nose. I ended up spending a week getting tested for all kinds of diseases because I refused to tell my mother that the bloody nose was the result of a *girl* punching me," Payson said, smiling and shaking his head. "And I had to bribe my brother to keep his big mouth shut. It cost me two rookie cards and my *Grand Theft Auto* time for a week."

"She knew. She told me a couple of years after we married. Remember when that patient in the ER clocked you a good one? Your eye looked horrible. She told me that if you had any more bruises, she was taking me to court for spousal abuse."

"She said what?"

"That she was keeping her eye on me," Jessie said with little emotion…now. She could almost laugh about his mother's comments. But there had been a bit of guilt that went along with it. She and Payson hadn't fought well. She certainly never hit him during their marriage, although the punch in high school had led to their first date because she'd felt so bad about giving him a bloody nose. That didn't mean that they didn't end up bruised and bloody when they argued during their marriage, it was just that no one could see the wounds.

"That explains the third degree when I saw her. Why didn't you say something?"

"It doesn't matter, Payson," Jessie said, wanting to steer away from their past. "Do you think you could talk with the physical therapists about the extra time? I don't understand why they don't have the material they need."

Payson didn't answer for a moment, and then said, "I really didn't know my mother thought that. If I had, I would have talked to her."

Their eyes caught. His gaze was direct and darkly intense. She could see that he was upset and wanted to make things right. It didn't matter now, Jessie told herself, and looked away. "About the physical therapists?"

"I'll talk with them," he said. They watched the children in the ring for a few moments.

"Thanks for getting the foundation to help Alex," she said. "He was so happy when I told him that he could keep coming. He's blowing the other kids out of the water, a total natural on a horse." Payson nodded in acknowledgment. "It's weird, though. Karin gave me a new billing address. I should probably call and confirm. That woman can be a little flaky."

"Give me the address," Payson said. "I'll confirm it. No problem."

"Okay," she said slowly.

She watched Payson focus again on the arena full of children. Her smile stayed in place despite her worries. Laughing with him had taken her right back to the days when she never questioned his love. The bond between them had made her feel so…secure, but that same feeling of security had always scared her. She had worried that in trying to make him happy, she would lose her independence. She shifted in her seat and Payson turned to her, a question on his lips, then his face tightened.

"What did I do now?" he asked, his brows lowered as he studied her face.

"I've got to go. I've got a lot to do. I don't have some cushy job at a hospital where I get a paycheck every week and someone cleans up all of my messes." She rushed away because she refused to get caught up in leaning on him ever again. He made that too easy.

JESSIE YAWNED AS she moved the ponies and horses into the corral. She couldn't wake up this morning, and it was Payson's fault. She'd woken three times from dreams of testing the strength of the bedsprings during their marriage. Jessie had only gotten a couple of hours of shut-eye. She'd been so sure that the sexual tension between them would disappear as she and Payson worked together and remembered all of the reasons that they weren't compatible.

Her increasingly erotic dreams showed her that, where Payson was concerned, she'd been wrong again. On edge and cranky, she'd exiled herself to hanging out with the animals after snapping at every single person she'd seen this morning. It had to stop. The problem was that she hadn't figured out exactly how to do that without kicking Payson off the ranch.

"IS THERE A reason that these forms have to be filled out tonight?" she asked as she leaned over the back of *her* office chair, occupied by Payson. He rapidly clicked around his spreadsheet.

"The committee needs a report by the end of the day tomorrow. I've got to get the stats together. So, yes, this needs to be done tonight. Could I have some room?" Payson asked as he rolled his shoulders. She could see the muscles shift under his golf shirt.

"I can't see the screen unless I stand here," she said to needle him a little.

"It doesn't make me fill this in any faster with you breathing down my neck."

"Well, it's a good thing I am breathing down your neck because that's not the figure for feed," she said, and leaned in a little more. Her breast tingled when it contacted his back. God, he smelled good. How could he smell good after a full day of work?

She stood up and moved away while she gave him the correct number. She paced in her small office as he typed. She was sure it wasn't worry about getting the numbers right that made him pound the keys. Like her, he must feel the arc of awareness that crackled between them.

She knew him well. She certainly recognized the narrow-eyed look he'd gotten when he stared at her breasts. When they were young and in love, that heated gaze would've led to the bedroom, where he would've tested his theories on how long a human body could stand to be teased. Jessie had begun to think that the current tension between them—left over from their marriage—came from remembering what was and reacting to each other instinctively. She'd been trying to ignore it. The tension hadn't gone away. It was getting worse, making her snappy and restless.

She knew that acting on the sexual connection, or whatever it was, would be a disaster. They had divorced for a lot of very good reasons. Maybe if they kissed for real, not just because she'd called him on his challenge, they would prove to themselves that what they remembered as amazing was actually ordinary. Before she talked herself out of it, she said, "Payson."

"Yes," he said but kept typing.

"Are you listening?" He nodded. "You know how you wait all year to go to the Pike's Peak Fair for the fry bread, and you keep thinking about it and no other fry bread tastes as good. Then you go to the fair and you eat it, but it doesn't taste all that good?"

"Let's just pretend I understand."

"What I'm saying is that you build something up in your mind as wonderful, as spectacular, but when you finally get it, it's really just ordinary." His head tilted, so she knew she had his full attention. "Well, you see, I've been thinking that maybe that's what's been happening here between us."

"I'm hungry for fry bread?"

"No," she said. She'd been an idiot to start this conversation. "You know, the tension, the remembering." He didn't say anything. "Maybe, if we kissed, we'd realize that it's not that special anymore. That all of that is behind us."

"You need to kiss me to prove to yourself…what?" he asked. He shifted in the chair and rolled his shoulders again, something he did when he was tense.

"I'm looking at this the way you would, like a scientist. We were married. We're not anymore, but we're working together. We're both remembering how it was, and it probably wasn't like we remember anyway. We need to prove to ourselves that there's nothing there. Nada."

"The theory that you'd like to test is that if we kiss, we'll discover that what we had was pretty ordinary?"

"Something like that. I'm just trying to be honest here. I know you feel the tension. I've seen those looks and I know what they mean. If we just kiss and get it out of the way, we'll be good to go. We'll have eaten the fry bread."

"When would you like to conduct this experiment?"

"What about now?"

"That will be fine. Let me input these final numbers and then I'll be ready," he said, his voice calm as he twisted to face the computer.

Jessie paced so she wouldn't stare at Payson and wouldn't think about what they were going to do.

"Okay. Done," he said. Had his voice cracked a little?

"Great," she said, laughing nervously. "I'm glad we're doing this. It will make working together so much easier."

When they were standing facing each other, the foot of space between them quickly heated. A barely there tremor started in her feet and quickly reached her breasts. He put his hands around her upper arms, pulling her toward him, but not against him. Her lips parted, anticipating what would come next. He hesitated. She shifted closer, and he finally leaned in, touching his lips to hers, softly, like a first kiss.

Jessie tried to stop the moan, but when her tongue touched his, the heat shot from her mouth into every inch of her body. She wanted more and clutched at his shoulders, trying to pull him closer. His hips brushed against hers and the kiss deepened. His hair was soft under her fingers as she held his mouth to hers. Then his lips were on her neck, in the one place that he knew would drive her crazy. She sucked in her breath and pressed herself against him. She didn't want him to stop. He nuzzled that sweet spot that only he knew. Just when she was going to push him away before she totally melted, he moved back to her lips, nibbling at the edges.

"You taste the same. How could you taste the same?" Payson asked softly, not pulling away.

"Hmm." She tried to get her brain working again. "The same toothpaste?"

He chuckled low and deep, holding her against him. "That could be." His mouth covered hers again, exploring her thoroughly. When he finally leaned back, he whispered, "Only you could make toothpaste sexy, Jessie." His hand roamed to the curve of her waist and the slight flare of her hips. "How can you be so soft? When I watch you walk, all I can think about is touching you. Will touching you now make me forget that?"

"Touch me," Jessie breathed. She used her mouth to explore his lips and spoke softly against his cheek, so he could feel her breath moving across his skin, "God, Payson, why would we want to forget this?"

"Jessie," he said, and let her go. She wrapped one long leg around the back of his knees to pull him back to her. He resisted for one second, then his fingers skimmed along her back as his mouth tasted her lips, her neck and her cheek.

When she thought she'd never take a full breath again and knew next they would be getting naked, she made herself take one step backward. They stood looking at each other, and she waited a moment for the space between them to cool.

She hoped when her brain—instead of her other parts—worked again, she'd figure out a way to see Payson every day and not remember this kiss, not remember that he tasted even better than on their long, slow wedding night. Jessie didn't need to be a genius like Payson to know that the kiss was the stupidest idea she'd ever had. Even worse than asking for Payson's help in the first place. She already craved his touch again. And, now, for the first time, she wondered why she'd filed for divorce when she still felt this sexual connection. Dang.

"So, what do you think?" Payson asked and then

cleared his throat. His voice had been thick and deep. "Did our experiment work?"

She tried to get her thoughts into a coherent string. "It might not seem like it now," she said, and stepped back to put more distance between them, "but can't you feel that, um, we didn't really have the same connection?"

"You're right," he said. "It was different."

"Yep. Totally different," she continued to lie. "Maybe we should call it a night. We proved our point."

Chapter Five

Jessie savored the quiet of the morning, needing to figure out how to respond to last night's "experiment." She'd been pushing back her first impulse to get mean and go on the attack, to hurt Payson before he hurt her. She knew he didn't deserve getting guff for agreeing to kiss her. She considered pretending that they hadn't kissed. As tempting as that was, pretending wasn't going to make the feelings go away. After exhausting every possibility while she tossed and turned, she'd accepted that the two of them needed to sit down and talk.

In the years since the divorce, Jessie had considered picking up the phone and calling Payson every so often. She didn't want to get back together or anything, but she wanted—needed—to apologize for a passel of nasty comments she'd made in those last months of their marriage. She also wanted to say sorry for blaming him for not coming to her right away at the Vegas hospital and that she forgave him—even if she maybe didn't completely—for not being with her when she needed him most.

The kiss was different.

She feared the memory of that one kiss would stick stubbornly in her brain forever. So what was she going to do? First, make sure that she and Payson weren't alone together—except she wanted to apologize and wasn't going to do that in front of an audience. Dang. She refused to call her mama or sister about this. They would tell her what she didn't want to hear, that she'd been crazy, stupid, idiotic to think the kiss was a good idea.

Jessie stumbled suddenly as a pony head butted her. She turned and with exasperated affection said, "Hey, Molly, how did you get out? I should have called you Houdini. Never knew a pony who was so good at escaping."

She took the little animal's halter and led her back to the pen she shared with Bull, a mean-spirited chestnut gelding that Jessie boarded for her brother. Bull was smitten with Molly but pretty much hated the rest of the world. If he was out, too, Jessie's morning would be really, really crappy—as if it wasn't already. She didn't want to wrestle the big horse back into his stall. Even with Molly around, he could be difficult. She hurried, her knee already aching with the thought of getting the cranky horse to cooperate. Maybe her brother should have named him Payson. She chuckled at that.

"You won't think it's funny if I let go of his halter," Payson said.

She clamped down hard on her tongue to stop a screech and said through clenched teeth, "What are you doing here? How did you catch Bull?"

"I wanted to speak with you before this place filled up with people. When I got to the barn, Molly was standing in front of this big guy. I grabbed him and she trotted off. I wasn't sure where she'd gone. I figured she'd taken off to find apples."

Jessie was stunned into speechlessness. First, Payson

had shown up looking for her after last night, and second, he'd voluntarily dealt with one of the horses, especially a troublesome one like Bull. "Molly was trying to keep Bull in? I figured she was the one trying to escape. She does it all the time when she's in the big corrals."

Payson shrugged and Bull leaned down and snuffled his hair. Payson pushed him away. Jessie waited for the horse to take off a finger. Nothing.

"Let me take him, and I'll get him and Molly back in their stall."

Jessie stepped forward and Bull immediately backed up, pulling Payson with him. The whites of the gelding's eyes showed. Jessie stopped moving before Bull got more upset. The horse immediately settled and stepped closer to Payson. "Let me take him," he said.

Jessie watched her horse-hating ex-husband lead Bull into his stall with Molly trotting after him like the sheepdog she thought she was. Payson gave each animal a hearty pat before he left them in the stall. Jessie stood and watched, speechless again.

"There are a few items we need to discuss," Payson said into the silence.

"Wait. What was that about?" Jessie said waving her arm in the direction of the stall. "You hate horses. When Candy Cane got out one night, and I asked you to help, you said that there was no way you were losing sleep over a 'dumb animal.'"

"Jessie, I was in the middle of my residency and had just come off a forty-eight-hour shift. I was exhausted. Plus Candy Cane always came back by morning. You used to say that she must have had tomcat in her because she liked to roam at night."

"When we lived out near Carefree that was fine. There

weren't any busy roads and people watched for critters. But then we moved to town so you'd have a shorter drive, which meant we were near a ton of major roads, including the 10. She wasn't used to that and could have gotten hit."

Payson didn't speak for a moment. "I'm sorry," he said, stunning her for a second time this morning. "I didn't even think about that. You had never worried before when she got out. I thought you were trying to punish me for missing your birthday."

She'd completely forgotten that. The week before Candy Cane went missing Payson and she had planned a nice evening to celebrate her twenty-fourth birthday. Then at the last minute he'd been called in to cover an extra shift. "I was upset that we didn't get to go out that night. It had been weeks since we'd spent any time together, but I understood. It wasn't your fault."

"That's not what you said. You said that if I had loved you, I would have said no to the shift. But I couldn't. The only time you could say no to shifts was if you were in the hospital yourself—in ICU."

"I said that? I'm sorry. I was being a real witch with a B, as Mama would say. Really, I barely remember the missed dinner," Jessie said.

"Amazing what sticks with you. We weren't as good at talking about our problems as we thought."

"Obviously. Or we wouldn't have gotten divorced," Jessie said. She felt the air suck out of the space between them, in anticipation of the blowup that would come after mentioning the big D. She stared at Payson, gauging his reaction. He looked thoughtful. "Sorry," she apologized again. "I shouldn't have…"

"Told the truth? We were so young—you'd just turned

nineteen when we got married," he replied as if that explained everything.

"My parents got hitched young, and they're still together."

"They were both rodeo people."

"No, they weren't. Mama met Daddy when he was riding in a show down in Texas. She was in her first semester at Texas A&M."

"Still, she was from a ranch family," Payson said.

"Yeah, but growing up on a small cattle operation isn't the same as raising horses and following the rodeo. Gram and Gramps barely spoke with her for years. Mama and Daddy were just as bad when we came back from Vegas. Mama said that we should just have lived together and not gotten married. I thought an alien had taken over her body because that was certainly not the woman who had raised me and insisted that living together was for sissies. She used to say that brave people got married."

"You didn't tell me that your parents weren't happy about us getting married."

Jessie took a deep breath. Another tricky bit of their shared past reared its ugly head. "I knew how upset your parents were. I thought dealing with them was more important. I knew Mama and Daddy would eventually be okay with us being married, as long as we were happy. I never thought that with your parents. I heard your mother threw a party when you were finally rid of that 'tacky rodeo girl.'"

"What?" Payson said. "She didn't throw a party."

His denial sounded less than truthful. She learned after a few years of marriage that nothing she did would satisfy Marquessa. The woman regularly made digs about everything, from Jessie's hair to her career. She'd told Jessie that she needed to act like a surgeon's wife, not "a vulgar circus tramp."

They stood for long minutes not talking, the silence not uncomfortable. The sadness of remembering what could have been tinged that space between her and Payson. Was it finally time to clear the air and get it all out there? He'd been right that they hadn't been so great at talking.

They were older now, but Jessie wasn't convinced she was any wiser. Talking about their past might show wisdom or be a big fat mistake, just like the kiss.

"Payson," Jessie started and felt the words freeze up in her throat. "I think we need to talk." He waited politely for her to continue. "Later. We don't have to do it today." She needed to work up to laying her heart open about the one day that had changed everything for her and for them. Plus, she'd only had one cup of coffee; she needed at least ten more to be up for this conversation.

"No. If you feel we need to have a conversation. Let's do it now."

"Next week will be fine." The idea of talking tightened the muscles in her throat, choking her, just as the tension moved to her neck and shoulders, shooting up into her head. She rubbed her temples.

His mouth worked and she braced herself for another demand. He surprised her when he said, "I'll make another pot of coffee. Maybe that will take care of your headache."

"Thanks." How had he known the pot was empty and she desperately needed more? An hour of cleaning stalls would help loosen the grip of the headache, too. Working in the barn had always been how she'd dealt with a problem. When they were married, she'd race out of the house and brush Candy Cane till the poor horse was nearly bald. Of course, Payson ran away, too, but saving a little kid's life sounded so much nobler than brushing a horse.

PAYSON WALKED INTO Jessie's office, ignoring the memory of their kiss as he concentrated on the coffeemaker. His mood lightened as he took comfort in how well he knew Jessie. She always had one cup of coffee before going to do her barn chores, chugged down like medicine to get the caffeine flowing. Then with the precision she'd perfected in her trick riding, she'd brew a full pot so its last drip fell into the carafe as she finished her work. Two or three cups into that pot and Jessie would finally be human. He could tell this morning that she hadn't had enough coffee yet, and on top of that, he'd seen the tension in her upper body that had made her rub at her temples. He knew she had a headache, which meant whatever she wanted to talk about was unpleasant. Her insistence, after bringing it up, that it could wait made him positive that the conversation she wanted to have centered on their shared past.

Talking would be a novelty for the two of them, since most the communication during their marriage had been nonverbal and between the sheets, which had gotten them into the bad habit of trying to solve their problems with sex. When they'd parted ways...not parted ways... when she'd walked out on him, he'd been fine with leaving their business unfinished because he never wanted to talk to her again. Ever. He'd shoved thoughts of her and their divorce into the same dark corner where he'd hidden the major reason for their breakup.

He watched the coffeepot's slow drip and decided he needed a mug, too. After last night's kiss, he'd barely slept, which is why he'd put that little experiment into his dark corner. He worried that his strategy would turn around and bite him in the butt. How could all of their baggage stay packed away when he worked with Jessie every day, stood next to her and felt the subtle heat of her body?

He glared at the slow drip. Who was he fooling? No dark corner would work for this. They needed to clear the air. Then they'd be able to move on—whatever the hell that meant. If it meant that he'd be able to start dating, he was all for it. Really. Since the divorce, he'd been living more or less like a monk—which now that he used his allegedly considerable brain power—he could directly link to his reaction to last night's kiss.

"Helen," he said into his phone after hitting speed dial. "I'll be running a little late. Can you push back my first two appointments?"

"That will mean you'll miss lunch."

"I'll grab a bite between patients." He pinched the phone between his ear and shoulder to pour coffee. The phone slipped and he missed what Helen said. He repositioned the phone. "What?"

"I said, I guess I'll grab a bite between patients, too."

"I'm sure I can handle the office for a half an hour so you can get lunch."

"No, it's fine," Helen said.

Payson knew that she didn't mean it was fine. When he got to the office, he'd convince her to take lunch. "I shouldn't be very late. I just need to clear a few things up here."

"You mean like why you and Jessie got divorced?" Helen asked shrewdly.

Payson stood with his coffee partway to his mouth.

Helen went on, "That's why you're going to be late?" A pause and he could hear the soft static of the connection. Helen gasped. "Payson MacCormack! Don't tell me you…"

"No," Payson protested, feeling his face burn. He added quickly, "If we did, I don't think it would be any of your business."

"You think it's none of my business? Who's the person who has to put up with you? Who's the person who has to explain to patients why Dr. Mac is grumpy like Oscar the Grouch? Hmm?"

"Reschedule the patients, please," he said carefully and ended the phone call.

He took a slug of coffee, hoping to God that the jolt of caffeine would get him through the unpacking of his baggage. For Jessie's coffee, he pulled the smiley mug out of the stack. Maybe it would put her in a better mood.

He found her at the entrance to the indoor arena with her phone pressed against her ear and frowning ferociously. Too far away to hear what she was saying, he hurried, a little worried that she might have gotten bad news about one of the children.

"You soulless…drone! We're talking about children's lives here," Jessie said into the phone, then listened for a moment. "Fine. I'll do that." She shoved the phone into her pocket and turned to start back to her office. He knew the second she spotted him. Her face went from fury to fear. "What are you doing out here?"

"Bringing you coffee. Is something wrong?"

"Why? What did you hear?"

"Not much, but you looked totally pissed off," he said, holding out the mug.

She took the coffee and stared into its depths. "Just a supplier who's being a pain. I'll work it out."

"Of course, Jessie the Lone Ranger never needs help from anyone."

"That's right," she said fiercely.

"Fine," he snapped, then took a deep breath. Rehashing a familiar argument would get them exactly nowhere. "We shouldn't wait to talk. I rescheduled two appointments. That will give us enough time to have the discussion we need to have in order for this—"

"Just like that? You set up a meeting and expect me to drop everything and rearrange my schedule?"

"We need to talk, and it can't wait, no matter what you said."

"Of course, Payson Robert MacCormack knows what's best and the rest of us should just fall in line."

"I never said that. But even you have to admit that we need to set parameters and metrics for the current relationship moving forward. We *cannot* have another incident like last night."

"Is it possible to get more pompous?"

"Ignoring problems doesn't make them go away."

"I know that. I'm not stupid."

"I never said you were stupid." He slowly unclenched his fists. No one else in the world could make him so mad so quickly. "An hour of your time will net us a workable rapport."

"Unlike you, I don't have a bunch of minions. An hour of my time right now isn't possible."

"You have volunteers and staff, Jessie. What specifically do *you* have to do that they can't?"

"First, there's all of that paperwork *you* people insist *I* fill out and then there are new students coming in today that I need to assess. It's my program. My people are good at following orders, but they can't take on new patients."

"That's not a sustainable operating procedure. You need to have a chain of command and cross training."

"I'm sorry that I don't live up to your standards."

Dear baby Jesus and his little angels, as he'd heard Jessie's mom say more than once. How had this conversation fallen off the rails? "That's not why I wanted to speak with you. The program is a separate issue—"

"Really," Jessie said slowly and with a touch of menace. "You think something is going on here, other than Hope's Ride and the hospital's endorsement?"

He'd never believed that people actually wanted to pull their hair out in frustration. Well, he'd been wrong, because he wanted to rip out every follicle right now. "Even you have to see that your little 'experiment' must be addressed properly…" As soon as the words left his lips, he knew he'd stepped into it.

"Again with the stupid."

He looked at the sky for divine intervention before his gaze dropped and landed on the parking area visible over Jessie's left shoulder. He sighed with relief. Keeping his voice neutral, he said, "*Your* people are here." Time to make a strategic retreat.

Chapter Six

"Jessie?" her sister, Lavonda, called from the door of a little-used barn where broken tack and old hay littered the floor.

"Yes," she answered after a moment more of sweeping. It was Friday, days after she and Payson didn't talk. If she could just get through the rest of the day, she knew that she'd be okay.

"I didn't want to say anything in front of anyone else, but I was the first one in today and found this on the front gate." She slapped a sheet of paper into Jessie's hand. "This is just a mix-up, right?"

Jessie glanced at the official-looking sheet and her heart stopped. She tried to smile reassuringly as she said, "Absolutely. Thanks for keeping this quiet. I just need to make a call, and it'll all be cleared up. Don't say anything to Mama and Daddy. It's nothing."

"If you say so," Lavonda said, giving Jessie a good long stare. "This program is amazing. Don't mess it up because you won't ask for help. These kids are getting better, because we're…you're…making a difference for them," she said with pride.

Lavonda had loved horses just as much as Jessie when they were little, but then she decided that rodeos and ranch life weren't for her. She'd gone off to conquer the corporate world but that didn't matter because now she was back home. Lavonda had told the family that she'd been given a great severance package and was taking time off to consider her options. Mama and Daddy had insisted she come to Hope's Ride. She hadn't shown up regularly, but she'd shown up. Of course she had to be here today of all days.

Jessie jumped when Lavonda gave her hand a squeeze. "We all want to help. We know how important your program is."

"Everything is fine."

"Jessie," her sister started. "I know you're a tough cowgirl, but even you—"

"Really. We're good."

"Saying it again and again doesn't 'make it so,' as Jean-Luc Picard would say."

Jessie smiled a little. She'd had a bit of a crush on Captain Picard, bald head and all. She and Lavonda had watched the show faithfully, even when they'd been on the road with Mama and Daddy. For a second or two, Jessie saw the little sister who'd won the junior bronc-riding championship and who never told when Jessie did forbidden riding tricks. The girl she'd shared a bedroom with, not the petite woman with the sleek bob and subtle makeup she was now, the kind of woman who'd have fit perfectly into Payson's family.

"I can't expect my family to step in every time I hit a little bump."

"First, that's what family's for. Mama always said so. Second, we're offering. Third, asking for help makes you stronger, not weaker." Jessie shook her head and Lavonda snorted, almost making Jessie laugh because she sounded a lot like Molly. "Let's take a walk down Memory Lane. Exactly how many times when you went it alone did it turn out well? That would be zero. Like when you bought your first trick horse by working yourself into a case of mono. Then the divorce—"

"We're not talking about that—"

"We wanted to help. We wanted you to lean on us sometimes. It makes it tough to come to you for help when you never ask for it yourself."

Lavonda's comment stopped Jessie's mouth. Could it be that being the strong, silent type didn't help her family and friends?

"Asking for help doesn't make you a failure. You know that now, right?" Lavonda asked seriously.

Her little sister's gaze stayed glued on her until Jessie wanted to squirm. "Sure," Jessie said with conviction she didn't feel because asking for help meant she couldn't do it on her own and if she couldn't do it on her own…then what?

"I can see the wheels turning by the smoke coming out of your ears. I won't tell Mama and Daddy about the paper because I'll believe you that it's a mix-up and that if you need help, you'll ask for it." Lavonda walked off without saying more, her slight form outlined by the sunlight coming through the barn door.

Jessie watched her sister for a moment, then refocused on what had been making her palms sweat in the dry heat. The foreclosure notice. She'd already received one, but that had been sort of a warning. That's the way the internet said it worked. She'd checked after she hadn't made the balloon payment. So even with this notice, she had weeks to come up with the money before the ranch would go up for auction. Her timeline for figuring out a better plan for saving Hope's Ride had been bumped up, that was all.

For a second, she considered speaking with Payson about the situation, but she didn't want him to solve her problems. They were divorced. He'd said that he didn't believe in the program, or something close to that. On the other hand, when they'd been married, sitting down and talking with him had made her feel steadier and better able to cope—at least, that was the way it'd been when they'd first married. She missed that part of being a couple. She'd gone to Payson to talk out her problems. She hadn't always followed his advice, which he had argued meant she wanted to do everything on her own.

And maybe he was right. The past three years had been tough because she'd refused to ask her family for anything beyond that first bit of money for the down payment on Hope's Ride. Her problems had been of her own making and she'd solve them on her own, just like now. Still, at times, she'd ached for Payson because she needed someone to lean on—just a little.

She spent the rest of the day avoiding Payson and an annoyingly deep-seated impulse to ask him for help with her bank problem. Next thing she knew, there he was. It was as though her thoughts had conjured him up. She kept up her slow sweeping.

"Jessie," Payson said sharply as he stepped closer. "You need to get out here and talk with these people."

"Who?"

"The Humane League is here and planning to take all of the animals," he said.

Sure he was needling her, Jessie looked over her shoulder to tell him to stick it where the sun don't shine. Then she saw his expression and bolted from the barn, running as fast as her knee allowed. The large parking area was overflowing with horse trailers. She approached the cluster of strangers in khaki uniforms. She could hear the children crying and adults shouting. Molly trotted around, loose again, nipping at men with ropes.

"Stop," Jessie yelled in a voice that easily carried over the noise.

"Miss Jessie," one of the teen riders came hurrying to her, followed by her staff and volunteers. They all talked at once, but Jessie zeroed in quickly on the important words: the Humane League had arrived to confiscate her ranch stock. She saw a woman who looked as if she was in charge near the gate. Jessie paused when she felt Payson's hand on her shoulder. "Let me call Spence," he said softly so no one else could hear.

"I didn't do anything wrong. I don't need an attorney," Jessie said, scared that he might be right about needing his brother's lawyering skills. "I'm sure this is all a mistake."

"Jessie, let me help."

She kept moving to stop herself from turning to him, leaning on him. She couldn't. This was her problem and her responsibility. She had to handle it. How would anyone, including Payson, take her seriously now if she didn't handle this? "Excuse me," she barked as she approached the woman with the clipboard and badge. "I'm Jessie Leigh."

The woman looked at her paper. "I'm looking for Jezebel Leigh MacCormack."

"That's me," Jessie said.

"I'm goin' to need to see ID before I present these papers. With all of these people riled up, I don't wanna get this wrong."

"Ask anyone here. This is my ranch and these are my animals you're stirring up."

Molly, on the loose again, squealed her displeasure. Jessie heard Bull bugling from his stall and pounding on the walls with his hooves. Stomps and snorts from other horses as well as barking from the two ranch dogs added to the deafening noise.

The woman in khaki didn't budge. "We're not trying to upset the animals. We're here for their welfare. I need your ID."

Jessie hurried to the house for her wallet. When she got back and handed her identification over, Jessie finally got to read the paperwork. Signed by a judge, the intent was clear. The Humane League had won the right in court to take the animals as "protection for their welfare."

"If you have any questions call our attorney. His name is on the documents. My job now is to help these animals," she said, trying to step away from Jessie. "Your cooperation would be appreciated, but it's not necessary."

"I don't understand why you're taking the animals. You can see that they're healthy. The vet is out here regularly. I have staff and volunteers to take care of the barns. Look at them. They're probably cleaner than the house."

Jessie's throat tightened in fear. She glanced at the papers again, searching frantically for the mistake. This had to be a mix-up. Maybe they'd inverted the numbers of the address.

The stiff-backed leader said, "You don't want me to have to call the sheriff, do you? Because if you obstruct our taking of the animals, that's what we'll have to do."

"You have no right. The animals are treated well. The

children rely on this program. If you take the horses, you'll set them back months. Can't you hold off until I can get this all cleared up?"

"I'm sorry. It's not my decision. Once I get the paperwork, it's my legal obligation to fulfill the order," the woman said. She wouldn't even look Jessie in the eye. Instead she nodded to one of the other Humane League workers.

Jessie tried again, "I'll talk to your attorney, whoever I need to. You can't take my animals."

"Ma'am," a burly man said as he walked up behind her. "We need you to step out of the way so we can do our work."

"Can't you do this later? You're upsetting the children. A lot of them are emotionally fragile," she said, trying to stay calm and keep her eye on the khaki crew.

"Ma'am," he said again and stepped closer. "We need you to step over here."

"No," she said. He wasn't the law. What could he do to her? She had to protect the animals and the children.

"Her attorney is on his way," Payson's authoritative voice cut through the din. "Until he arrives and can thoroughly review the paperwork, you are trespassing, according to Section 125 of the Arizona property seizure code. He suggests that you wait in the public right-of-way at the end of the drive."

She'd never admit it, but relief overwhelmed her when Payson stepped in to help. She kept her mouth clamped closed on anything that might come spewing out.

"I've never heard of Section 125," the woman in charge said.

"Obviously or you would not be so blatantly violating it," Payson said. He stared the woman in the eye as he spoke. It only took a moment for her to turn and walk back to the others. They all got in their vehicles and moved to the end of the lane. As soon as the dust settled, Jessie walked to the cluster of children and adults. She explained in a bright, firm voice that there had been a mix-up and it might take some time to straighten out. Then she had to tell them that therapy was canceled for the day and possibly Monday. A stab of pain and guilt went through her as children cried or turned red and yelled in fury. With the help of the shocked adults, Jessie got all of the children into their cars and on their way. She was aware of Payson talking with the youngsters and answering his phone, working alongside her the whole time.

With all of the children on their way and the Humane League at the end of the drive, Jessie took a deep breath for the first time in half an hour. She had to gather herself to speak with the staff and volunteers. She also needed to talk with Payson and find out if Spence was really on his way and what blood money his brother would expect. She'd never been Spence's favorite person. First, she had to get her feet to move, to carry her toward the milling group of men and women who believed in Hope's Ride, too.

"Jessie," Payson said quietly. "Spence'll be here as soon as he can."

"Is there really a Section 125?"

"Not exactly. Spence figured it would slow them down until he could get here and see exactly what the paperwork said."

"Oh."

"Maybe you should talk with everyone," Payson said,

speaking soothingly. "They need assurance. It'll be fine, Jessie. Spence'll figure something out."

She wanted to snap at him to stop treating her like a crash victim. She didn't want to need his soothing words, but she did. His touch, the sound of his voice steadied her. Beside Payson, she found the guts to step toward the small crowd. She explained that an attorney was on his way and everything would be taken care of as soon as possible. She asked them all to get the horses and ponies comfortable and then head home.

The end-of-the-day chores were nearly done when a big diesel-burning Ford F-150 came roaring into the yard.

"There's Spence," Payson said and walked to the truck before the dust had settled. "Thanks for coming."

"No problem, pardner," Spence said. As tall as Payson, but broader through the chest, he looked like an ad for an all-American blond male with his dusty blue eyes and hint of a dimple. "Let me get on my workin' clothes." He reached into the cab for a cowboy hat and a Western-style jacket. He was as much a cowboy as Payson was. She didn't know him well. He'd been a couple of years behind them in school and then gone East to college. After their marriage, Payson and Jessie were not exactly the MacCormacks' favorite guests. But the one thing she did know about his family was that nothing they did came cheap. No way could she afford Spence, and she could hardly expect a family discount.

"Jessie, can you get the paperwork they gave you?" Payson called to her.

"It's been a long time, but you're still the same Jessie. Gettin' my brother deep into it." She stiffened, ready to tell him to take a flying leap, then, like an unpredictable stallion, he switched tactics. "Now, I hate to cut the reunion short, but they did give you papers, right?"

Before she could open her mouth, Payson answered, "Maybe it would be best if you just went and talked with them?"

"I could do that." Spence squinted down to the end of the drive. "Get any paperwork you think I need, and I'll be back directly."

Spence sauntered toward the group from the Humane League, his boots making small puffs of dust. Payson said, "He's either been in Texas too long or he's been watching a *Justified* marathon."

"What?" Jessie asked, trying to take in what had just happened.

"He picked up the whole damned cowboy thing when he was in Texas. He says it puts his opponents off their game."

"Texas ain't Arizona," Jessie said, and then got to the meat of the problem. "I can't afford him. I can only guess what he charges."

"Forget about the money. Let me help you," Payson said, obviously exasperated.

Everyone needed help. Isn't that what she told the kids all of the time? Isn't that what Lavonda had said to her? Accepting any help from Payson, though, had always been a painful balancing act. When they'd married, she'd had so little and he'd already had so much. She had wanted him and his family to respect her. In her world, people got respect by standing on their own two feet. "Thanks for calling Spence," Jessie said quietly. "I'll pay you back. It may take a while, though. Keep track."

She watched his full mouth tighten, then he looked

over her shoulder. "Here comes Spence. Hopefully, he's gotten it all straightened out."

Payson's brother looked from one to the other and adjusted his hat. "Well, there does seem to be a problem. They have an order to place the livestock and all other domestic animals in preemptive protective custody. It seems to be a new tactic the Humane League is taking when properties go into foreclosure." By the end of the brief speech, the good-old-boy drawl was gone, and he stared at her hard.

"Foreclosure," Payson repeated.

"I'm working on that," she said, forcing steel into her voice.

"Working on it?" Payson asked, his voice deepening. "How exactly? You barely charge anything for your therapy but pay top dollar to your staff. You take in any damn animal that someone wants to get rid of. How exactly are you taking care of it?"

"It's not your problem, Payson," she barked. She didn't need to have him point out that she was a bad businesswoman.

"It certainly is my business. If I don't take care of you, who will? Huh?"

"You don't need to take care of me. You never did."

Payson's anger had been squarely aimed at the Humane League until he'd found out about Jessie's part in this farce. Foreclosure. Not a word from her or a peep about needing help, of course.

"You two settle your divorce on your own time," Spence said sternly, breaking into Payson's thoughts. His brother's gaze stayed glued on Jessie. "When did you get notice of foreclosure?"

"This morning."

"Just this morning?" Spence asked with doubt lacing his voice.

"There was another note, but I'm sure I can work something out. I've done it before and I'm not behind by a lot. Last time I got behind, I paid a little and got more time. I'm sure I can get another partial payment to them. I did internet research. I've still got time."

"I want to see the original mortgage. They've been slipping in extra language. You should have called me to look at it…or called someone. Who the hell knows what you signed away."

Payson looked at Jessie, her chin thrust forward and her hands on her hips. Spence was right. Now was not the time to argue. Hope's Ride had become his problem when he agreed to lead Desert Valley's team. The program and his career were at stake.

With the Humane League on the doorstep because of the foreclosure, the first order of business was getting rid of the foreclosure, which meant paying enough to the bank to get them to back off. Spence could take care of that. It would be up to Payson to get Jessie to accept help in the form of cash.

"We don't have a lot of time here," Spence said. "That group at the end of your lane wants to 'protect your animals.' I have a call in to the judge who made the order. I'm going to work on getting an injunction. I'm not sure how that will go."

Payson heard Jessie take a shaky breath. He didn't think he could handle it if she started to cry. He never could, not that she let herself cry very often. "Jessie, why don't you take Spence to your office to get him the paperwork?" He didn't wait for her to answer but shooed the two of them toward the barn.

When they left, he convinced the staff and volunteers still hanging around to go home. Fortunately, the hospital's employees had gone for the day, or they'd be no way for Payson to keep this quiet and get it cleared up without screwing up Jessie's chances for a hospital affiliation along with his own career. He stood by himself, long after the last vehicle was just a plume of dust.

He had to get the money, then talk Jessie into accepting the cash, all while making sure the hospital didn't get wind of the problem until after it was solved. He started damage control with the hospital by getting Helen involved. He told her that if she got phone calls, she needed to be clear that the Humane League visit had been routine, and any rumors about money should be blamed on a mix-up at the bank, which had been addressed.

Helen balked. He made it clear to her—just as it was clear to him—that saving Hope's Ride was the only way to save his own career.

Reluctantly, Helen agreed to help, ending the call by saying, "Don't forget what's important here—and it's not fixing everything."

"I have a mother, thank you," he snapped and walked behind one of the outbuildings so Jessie and Spence wouldn't find him while he called his investment adviser. His parents were well-off but had never been as wealthy as Jessie imagined or they pretended. Plus, Payson had, like Jessie, wanted to strike out on his own. He'd gotten a small trust when his grandmother died, but any money he had now he'd earned. His bank account was healthy but not unlimited, plus he'd been subsidizing

Alex's treatment at Hope's Ride until the hospital affiliation would get his insurance company to pay.

He could scrape together enough for the bank—he hoped anyway—but he would need time to sell off stocks. Once he had the money, though…anyone else would just thank him for the help. Jessie might just kick him off her property. Her independence had attracted him when they were young. When so many other girls had been interested in the gifts he could buy them, she'd told him to not "waste money on flowers that'll die anyway." The only jewelry she'd ever worn had been the plain wedding band. No diamond engagement ring because it'd "just get dirty and caught on stuff."

He'd still wanted her to know how important she was to him and how much he loved her. So to celebrate their short engagement, he'd bought her a big sleigh bed she'd fallen in love with at an art co-op. It was fancifully painted with hearts and pairs of wild animals and a very modestly covered Adam and Eve. It had barely fit in their apartment's bedroom, but it had been worth the bruised knuckles when his cowgirl had cried seeing it for the first time in their home. Next thing he knew, they were lying on the bed, snuggled together as she kissed him and told him how much she loved him…and the bed.

He knew the ranch was even dearer to her than that bed, but that wasn't why he'd save the damned place. What was important was protecting his career by making sure the time and money the hospital had spent so far wouldn't be wasted. Next step to achieving his goals? Come up with an argument so persuasive that Jessie couldn't say no to his money. Or…he could just lie.

Chapter Seven

Jessie listened as Spence spoke with the judge on his phone and her stomach churned faster. She paced her small office, hoping the movement would soothe her, or at least keep her mind occupied. Right now, it yelled "loser."

Her breath caught every time she pictured Molly being dragged away. What about Bull? She had to call her brother and get him to come over for his horse. There were three other animals that technically belonged to others. Jessie boarded them in exchange for using them in the program. Where was her cell? She had to call them. The Humane League couldn't have those horses. She headed to the door and stopped when she saw Payson.

"What?" she asked, her voice shakier than she expected.

"Nothing," he said, but his gaze didn't quite meet hers. "Has Spence talked with the judge?"

She gathered herself, trying to push fear aside. "He's on the phone now." If she didn't say that it was going badly, everything would be fine. "I should make some calls, too." She tried to move past him.

"I need to talk with you."

"It's going to have to wait," she said.

He captured her arm and said, "It's about this mess you've gotten yourself into."

"Thanks for your understanding and support." She didn't need him telling her she'd messed up. She knew that.

"It *is* a mess," he said, defensively. "And, of course, you're going to be unreasonable about it."

"Unreasonable because I don't want a bunch of hopped-up do-gooders taking my animals?"

"You didn't tell me you were in trouble," he said, an edge she'd rarely heard entering his voice.

"I wasn't until today. And I've let you help. Who called Big Bad Spence? You. And why would I tell you about anything? We're not married."

He put a little space between them. "I thought we were at least colleagues, maybe even friends. The fact that you were on the brink of foreclosure is something you should have shared, especially with my hospital involved."

She understood, but she said, "I didn't because Hope's Ride is *mine*."

"Hey," Spence's voice interrupted. "I'm on the phone. Take it outside."

Jessie wanted to point her finger at Payson and tattle that it was all *his* fault. Instead, she took the adult route, turned and left the office. She needed a few minutes to herself anyway. A snack would get her thinking more clearly so she could figure out who she needed to call. She hunched her shoulders and looked down as she walked to the house, expecting Payson to hurry after her. She tried to decide if she was happy that he'd left her alone. She had to remember that he was only in it for the title.

Inside, she hurriedly got a soda and tortilla chips. The small but cozy ranch house suited her with its warm, desert-sunset tones and comfortable, rustic furniture. She also took time to rinse her face, retie her hair and put on a clean shirt. It made her feel refreshed and ready to face the people at the ranch's entrance. She didn't need Big Bad Spence. She would just talk to the group. They would have to see that she cared about the animals and would never abandon them, no matter what happened to the ranch. She veered away from that thought.

The scream of a power tool biting into wood broke her concentration. Who would be working at the ranch today? No one. They'd all left. Had Daddy driven all the way from Tucson to do "repairs"—his code for checking up on her? Of course, he'd have to pick today to stop in.

Jessie tried to open the front door, concocting the story she'd tell her father to explain the khaki brigade at the end of the drive and the lawyer in her office. She looked down at the doorknob in her hand that didn't turn. The power tool had quieted, and now she heard the grumble of a male voice.

"Daddy," she yelled through the door. No response. "Daddy?" Well, heck, he was probably listening to his iPod. She went to the back door, yanked it open and screamed. A stranger was standing at *her* door holding a circular saw.

Not moving the blade, he said, "What are you doing in the house? No one's supposed to be in the house."

"It's my house. Get off my property before I call the police."

"This is the bank's property," he said, giving her a stern look.

"I'm calling the police," she said, turning back inside. She heard static as Saw Man spoke into a bright yellow walkie-talkie. She hesitated. The adrenaline from the scare had drained away and her mind cleared. What had he said about the bank?

"Jessie," Payson called from the front porch.

She looked at the back door again but Saw-Man had disappeared.

"Jessie," Payson said again, a little louder.

"Coming," she answered, taking three deep breaths and hoping her snack stayed in her stomach. On the porch, Payson stood with two men dressed in gray uniforms. A heavy engine growled and she saw a large tow truck backed up to her garage. She started off the porch, but Payson's hand on her arm stopped her.

"They told me that the mortgage company sent them out. How long have you known about the foreclosure?" he asked, his voice tight and very low.

She could barely hear him over the noise of the nearby truck. The men in the uniforms looked away. "I gave you the paper from today. This can't be right. The internet article said that it takes at least 120 days."

"Give me the paper again," Spence said, having popped up behind his brother.

Jessie dug in the pocket of her jeans and pulled out the crumpled paper. Somewhere between scared witless and weeping mad, Jessie held it together. She stepped closer to Payson as Spence read quickly. The starchy scent that she'd always associated with Payson steadied her. She had four months to find the money to make the loan right, before it could go to foreclosure. She *knew* she had time, so what were these yahoos doing? She raced to the barn to tell the tow-truck driver to keep his hands off her Scout—the truck she adored even though it had been built before she was born.

In the doorway, facing the tow truck, Spence caught up to her and said, "Found the problem. This is not the first notice. When did you get the other one? They have it that the house is being sold next week."

"What? They can't do that."

"The order for this repo team is what triggered the visit from the Humane League. But there are other complications."

"This makes no sense. The first one was just a prelude, right? I'm sure that's what the article said. One notice and I'd have 120 days after the second notice." Jessie stood for a moment, then asked hopefully, "So, we can just tell them to leave, right?"

"Even if there was a problem with the notices, there's another complication."

"Lay out exactly what we're looking at here, Spence," Payson said from somewhere behind her.

"Come over here," Spence said, leading them to a piece of shade near one of the outbuildings. "I've got to be quick or they'll clean you out."

Jessie stiffened and her heart stopped. She didn't shake off Payson's hand when he laid it on her arm.

Spence said, "The judge who initiated the proceedings is off sick and it's Friday afternoon. That means all the other judges are on their way out the door, and they don't want to hear anything that will keep them a second past five o'clock."

Payson's hand slid down and took hers as he leaned

forward just a little and said to Spence, "What are you going to do about this?"

"This is like facing the firing squad. Take a step back. I'm just telling you how it is. You can't expect miracles here."

Jessie pulled her hand away from Payson's. She turned away as she said, "What *can* you do?"

"I'll show the guys messing with the locks that the sale doesn't take place for a week and that you are occupying the home. It's not abandoned as I'm guessing they assumed. That will get them to call their bosses at least. They don't want to get sued. I'll show the same thing to the Humane League. We should be able to put everything on hold until we can get a judge to straighten this out next week, or we have time to negotiate with bank and the mortgage company. That's the best case, anyway."

"What the hell, Spence," Payson burst out. "That's the best you can do? That *maybe* they'll listen?"

"You need to step back, Doc," Spence said. "I will do my job, that's why you called me. You two go to the office and stay there while I straighten this out. You'll just make it worse."

Jessie wanted to protest, but she couldn't see the easy-going cowboy anywhere on Spence's face or in his stance. In its place was a stone-faced man she wouldn't want to mess with. Payson followed her to the barn and her quiet office.

PAYSON TOOK A SECOND to enjoy the cool darkness of the barn and stopped Jessie before they got to the office. "Next time there's a problem, you need to come to me. We're supposed to be partners on this project."

"I've tried really hard to work with you, but you've all made it clear that all you're worried about is the 'data to prove the metrics.'"

"You're the one who asked the hospital…asked *me* for help," Payson said and Jessie stiffened. "I don't want to take over your program permanently. I just need you to communicate—"

"That's funny coming from you."

"What does that mean? You've always been the silent cowboy or cowgirl or whatever. Your parents talk all of the time. I never understood it."

"Maybe because you never listened," she said, leaning forward.

He leaned in, too, seeing the sun streaks in her hair. "I listened. I just didn't agree. You never wanted my help. You had to 'stand on your own two boots.'"

"Because you always thought you knew better. I talked to the doctor about my riding. He said it was fine, and when I told you that, you know what you said? Do you? 'Give me his number. I don't believe you.'"

"Because then, just like now, you only told me half of what was going on. Like how sick you were. I only knew because I found the medicine hidden in our underwear drawer."

"I could handle it—"

"You always said that you could handle it, even when you couldn't, and when I or anyone else offered to help, you just walked away or lied or—"

Spence interrupted, "Bad time?"

Payson shut his mouth tight and hoped his brother hadn't heard much of the argument. And if he had, that he'd keep quiet about it. Payson fidgeted with change in his pocket as he waited for Spence to continue.

"Lucky for you, I've got a trustworthy face. The Humane League agreed to post the warning until the actual sale or the bank/mortgage company stops the foreclosure, whichever comes first. The repo crew said that they couldn't make any decisions 'in the field.' I got them to allow Jessie to keep her equipment. Sorry. Getting a text," Spence said looking at his phone and then talking quickly. "They're changing the locks on the house. You are forbidden to enter, but no items will be removed."

"Where am I supposed to stay?" Jessie asked, her voice rising.

"A hotel," Spence said, his gaze glued to his phone.

"If I had the money for a hotel, I wouldn't be in foreclosure," she said.

"Stay with your family. That's what you did when you and Payson fought," Spence said shortly, his gaze not moving from the phone's screen.

"I don't want Mama and Daddy to know about the problem. They would want to help, and they've already done enough. If I stay with Lavonda or Danny...I don't want them to have to lie to our parents."

Spence shrugged.

"You can stay at my place," Payson said without thinking.

"Perfect," Spence said. "See you, bro." His brother didn't stop to say anything to Jessie or apologize. His eyes went back to his phone as he strode out of the barn. Had Spence always been like this with Jessie?

That didn't matter now. Payson needed to act fast before Jessie got her feet under her and went from stubborn to intractable. Her pale face told him that the shock of the afternoon hadn't left her. He might have just enough time to get her packed up and off to his house. His gut suddenly tightened and uneasiness settled into his shoulders. "Damn," Payson said involuntarily.

"What?"

"It's quiet," he said. She just looked at him. "The repo guys have left and the house has a new set of locks."

They stood for a moment, looking at each other, and Payson saw exactly when the lightbulb went on for her. "My clothes are in there. And my wallet." She hurried toward the house, the usual hitch in her step more pronounced.

Payson followed her, three steps behind, catching up outside the one-story house. "You can't go in there. You heard Spence."

"What good has he done? They still kicked me out of my house, and they're going to take my animals."

"He's not a miracle worker. If you had told someone sooner…" He closed his eyes, cursing himself and her. How could she push him into saying such stupid things?

Jessie glared at him, the brightness of tears glinting in her eyes.

"It's a bad situation, Jessie," he said softly, wanting to reach out and comfort her. But he didn't have the right, and even if he did, she would push him away.

"I thought I had it all figured out. With the hospital endorsing the program, I could get an extension on my credit. Then it wouldn't take me long to make up any payments. It just wasn't happening fast enough. Everyone took so much time."

"I'm sorry." He surprised himself by meaning it. He certainly hadn't meant for this to happen.

She looked surprised, too, then her face settled into determined lines. "I bet I can get in through the back window," she said.

"No. You're not breaking into the house and getting into more trouble. We'll stop on the way to my house and pick up a few things."

"I'll sleep in the barn. I've done it before."

"I'm sure you have. But you're not doing it tonight."

"Payson, I am not coming to your house."

"Where else are you going to go? You said you won't call your parents, and you don't want your brother and sister lying about what's going on." He planted his feet, placing himself in her way. "It's just for a night or two. I have a spare room. No big deal."

"No big deal," she repeated.

She looked so lost and vulnerable that he wanted to take her to his house, tuck her into bed and feed her soup. He'd feel that way for anyone who was getting kicked to the curb like Jessie was. "Spence really is a good attorney. I bet you'll end up only staying at my place one night," he said as cheerily as he could manage, while his gut roiled at the sight of her slumping shoulders.

"Keep the receipts for the clothes and stuff. I'm going to pay you back."

His first impulse was to tell her that she was being ridiculous. He could afford clothing and toiletries. Instead, he said, "Absolutely, and when Hope's Ride is world famous, you're taking me out for a steak dinner."

Chapter Eight

As Payson listened to his shower running, he pulled containers from the freezer and stared at them hard so he wouldn't picture Jessie, down the hall and naked...

Salad. He had to have salad. Greens were important to have in the diet. He pulled a covered bowl from the fridge and sniffed. Nah. The mix of arugula and endive was way past when anyone should eat it. Memories of the nights that he'd fixed food for the two of them popped into his brain. He'd always liked putting together meals. Good thing, too, because Jessie's idea of cooking had been eggs. That was it. Anything else came in a cardboard box or a bag from a fast-food place. Of course, in the beginning, food hadn't been at the top of his priority list for what made a good marriage. At the heart of the relationship, for him and for Jessie—back then—had been what happened in their big fanciful bed.

He looked up at the condo's ceiling, the blank whiteness erasing the images that raced through his mind. The water stopped. He froze. She'd be out looking for her dinner in minutes. Time to stop the trip down Memory Lane and concentrate on now. Jessie was just a professional colleague. He'd worked with numerous women and never thought about them in bed.

Fix the damned dinner.

He turned back to the chili that Helen had given him in her need to take care of him. *That's right, concentrate on the food.*

Helen treated him like one of her wayward children, which made him smile a little. He rummaged in the cupboard and found a half-filled bag of tortilla chips. That would have to be good enough for tonight. Exactly the kind of meal he'd made when they'd been married. *Nope. Not thinking about that again.*

He heard the scuff of bare feet on the hallway tiles and looked up to see a wet-haired Jessie. "Feel better?" he asked, gesturing for her to sit at the bar that separated the small kitchen from the living area.

She nodded and he looked at her more closely, noting her red eyes. She must have gotten soap in them, he told himself. "Dinner will be ready in a sec." He handed her a longneck bottle of beer.

"Can I help? Set the table or anything?"

"I've got it," he said. "Sit down."

Jessie sipped her beer and finally sat when he set the bowls of food on the bar. They ate in silence for a few minutes.

"Nice place," she said.

"It's a five-minute drive to the hospital."

She nodded. They were silent again. Payson wanted to say something, talk about anything, but he wasn't sure what. Maybe the weather?

Jessie said, "Thanks again for the clothes and everything. I'll be out of your hair tomorrow. I'm sure Spence will have the repo guys straightened out by then."

Since tomorrow was Saturday, Payson was just as sure nothing would happen, but he kept quiet.

"Alex is doing well, isn't he?" Jessie asked, obviously trying to start a conversation.

Payson thought this might be a safe topic. "He's been more compliant about his other therapies recently. That's helping."

"Doesn't he have a new therapist?" She sounded truly interested.

Payson told her about the woman working with Alex now. From there, they spoke about the other children and by then, the dishes had been put in the dishwasher. He suggested they go out to the patio. He would have suggested watching TV, but the only seating in his living room was the couch. Sitting with Jessie there would be much too intimate.

He ushered her into the small outdoor space, enclosed by plants and a wooden lattice that made it private and, at night, really, really dark. He'd never been out here at night. He usually sat on the patio in the morning and had his coffee. "I'll get a candle," he said.

"No, it's fine. There's plenty of light."

He didn't think so, but she lived out of town where nights were a lot darker. The air was warm, and he could hear the hum of the traffic from the nearby interstate. Payson took a sip of his coffee. He needed the jolt of caffeine so he could do more work after Jessie settled for the night. He told himself firmly to stay focused on "professional colleague." No remembering her in bed, hair mussed, lips swollen from his kisses.

"So Spence moved to Texas?" Jessie asked eventually.

Payson nearly spilled his coffee as he jerked to attention. His mind had wandered again where it shouldn't have. The dark hid the guilt and embarrassment, but couldn't stop his voice from cracking with tension when he said, "For about a year, for a big case with his law firm, right after he got married."

He could see the vague outline of her head nod. "How is his wife? And how's their little boy?"

"He and Missy are divorced." He was reluctant to say anything about his nephew, Calvin. Spence was his brother, not the parent of a patient, so it wasn't exactly a doctor-patient confidentiality thing—but Spence had asked Payson's opinion on the boy's doctors and their treatments. Seeing Spence try to work out visits and care while his son lived with Missy two hours away had made Payson think hard about what would have happened to him and Jessie. Definitely not the time—or place—to dig up old hurts. Still, he couldn't stop himself from asking in the anonymity of the dark, "Do you think we would have made it? If you hadn't lost the baby." Jessie didn't say a word or move. He fumbled to fill the quiet.

The baby…

"I don't know why I asked that," he whispered. "Too much beer?"

"She was *our* baby," she said stiffly.

"I know," he said as the agony of loss came back at him in a rush.

"The doctor told me it was okay to ride. If she'd told me to stop, I would have."

"I talked with the hospital's director of obstetrics. He said there was a risk—"

"Of course there was a risk, but there was also a risk with driving and a risk walking down the stairs."

"Jessie," he stopped, not sure what else to say. He wanted her to say what? That he was right? How would that make anything better? It wasn't as if they could bring back their baby or repair their marriage.

"I've gone over everything from that day again and again," she said into the inky silence. "I've tried to understand what could have gone wrong..." She paused for a moment and he heard her swallow. Even in the dimness, he saw the pale blur of her hand swiping at her eyes. "What I could have done to stop it. It's not so bad now, but right after I got out of the hospital in Vegas, that's all I could think of."

"Why didn't you say something to me? We could have talked with a doctor to figure out what happened." Instead, he'd stewed, almost convincing himself—in his blackest moments—that she'd kept riding because she didn't want the baby.

"Why would I talk with you about our baby?" Another tense pause and she added thickly, "All you could say was that you told me so."

"I never said that," he said, collapsing back into his chair under the weight of her accusation.

"You were always telling me what to do, how to improve myself. I never felt like I was good enough," she said with a catch in her breath.

"That wasn't the way it was," he said. Had he really treated her that badly? He'd loved her. He couldn't imagine that if he loved her, he would have said things like that. She had been the one who held back. She'd rejected him, rejected his help again and again, always wanting to do things on her own. He never felt like she really needed *him*. Was it that she hadn't understood that he was a man and men fixed things, no matter if they were a cowboy or a doctor?

"You did think I was good enough for one thing... sex. When we got home from Las Vegas, after...all you wanted to do was get me into bed," she accused. The tears and fury in her voice didn't need any light to be clear, even to thick-headed him.

"Not right away, but as soon as the doctor said we could. I wanted to comfort you," he said, knowing even as he said it that it was lame. But that was what he'd been trying to do, and a small, deep-down part of him had probably thought that replacing the lost baby with another would make them both feel whole again. He hadn't been thinking straight, and his unintentionally thoughtless actions and words had wounded the woman he loved.

JESSIE DREW IN a breath, trying to slow her racing heart. The pain of remembering the baby, remembering that time, made it hard to breathe. She gasped a little to get enough air, trying to figure out if she wanted to go on or stop right now. She opened her mouth, closed it, drew another shallow breath and said, "When you didn't come right away, I named our baby Violet. All on my own. I wanted to see her, and you weren't there to make them let me see her." She tried to breathe in and couldn't. The rush of sadness and anger overwhelmed her, just as it had when Payson had finally shown up by her bedside in that sterile, icy-cold hospital room in Vegas. "They kept telling me you were coming and you didn't. I needed you, and you weren't there."

"I couldn't just walk away, I was in the middle of holding some boy's guts together," he said. He sounded truly upset.

"You should have. Violet was our baby. She needed you. I needed you."

"I got away as fast as I could."

"How could I have forgotten that your wife and child

were nothing compared to your career? To being a doctor." She'd finally said it out loud when he could hear it. The dimness of the patio made it easy to talk. "I wasn't important, and our marriage certainly wasn't as important as doing some surgery or working an extra shift at the hospital."

"We talked about how it would be when I went to med school."

"Yeah, well, I guess I didn't really understand what that meant," she said, and quickly added, "I don't mean the missed dinners. I mean that *everything* came in second to being a doctor. You never asked about how the shows were going or even how I was feeling, what I might be planning for *my* career. Then when I told you I was pregnant, do you know what you said? 'Good. You'll finally stop all of that rodeo crap.' Not one comment about being happy that we were having a baby."

"I said the first stupid thing that came into my head. I was so overwhelmed, and I don't remember you saying you were happy about the pregnancy, either. I do remember you telling me that there was *no* way you were giving up riding. You said pioneer women did it all the time."

Jessie didn't answer him right away. She wanted to gather her thoughts and her emotions. She had said all of that—or close enough. Now here she was, sitting across from Payson, the man who'd broken her heart *and* made her the happiest she'd ever been in her life. It was time. She had to tell him what she'd been bottling up for the past three years.

"I was freaked out, Payson. Afraid of having a baby and what that would mean for my life, and scared because I knew the baby would be my responsibility. You were never around. I could see that medicine would always be the most important thing in your life. So much in my life was going to change. I couldn't give up my career, too. I worried about the baby. I did ask the doctor about riding, and I did modify my tricks. I wanted Violet. Even though I knew that you didn't really want the baby and I didn't know how I could make everything work, I wanted her."

"How could you say that you were alone? We were married."

"But did we really have a marriage? I don't remember sitting down and talking about anything important like having children or how we were saving for retirement. It seemed like we were either arguing about our schedules or in bed making up."

Payson sat quietly. Even his chest barely moved with his breathing. Jessie wondered if she'd said too much and he'd decided he'd had enough.

"We did talk," he said at last. "I remember talking with you about the amount of time it would take for me to be a doctor. I remember telling you how important it was to me. I remember saying that a piece of me would always be missing if I didn't become a doctor. It was the only thing I'd ever wanted to do, to be. I found an accelerated program in pediatric surgery. I knew it would mean a lot less time together in the beginning, but the plan was that we'd make up for it later. What about you? You were with the rodeo and never home. When you were home, you were rehearsing or taking care of the animals."

Jessie clicked her teeth together to stop herself saying a string of nasty words. She wanted to have a different conversation. They'd been sharing new details, but they were having the same argument: my career, my needs are more important than yours. "Thank you for wanting to get through the program quickly, but you should have talked with me about it and been honest about what that would mean for our marriage. You never told me that you would be away from the house for days or that when you got home, you'd be so exhausted that all you would do was sleep or bark at me."

"I never imagined it would be as bad as it was. I knew it would be a lot of hours, but there were times that it was insane. I considered quitting once or twice because I knew what it was doing to us."

"You never said a word," she said, astounded by the revelation. "I thought you enjoyed being away, that you were tired of being married to someone like me. You would talk on the phone with other people in the program and you laughed. When we talked, which was almost never, you gave me orders or grunted like a caveman. The only time you wanted to be around me was when we were in the bedroom."

"It would have gotten better if you'd just stuck it out."

"It wasn't me who checked out of the marriage. It was you. *You* stopped loving me. I *never* stopped loving you," Jessie said, the words coming from deep inside her, from a place where she'd been so wounded that until that very moment she hadn't been able to say how she felt.

"Don't ever say that," he whispered. "I would have done anything to stay together. *You* were the one who divorced *me. You* walked out on *me*…on us."

"I had to," she said. "I had a lot of time to think while I lay in the hospital after…Violet. I tried to imagine what the baby's life would have been like. She would have known you as the guy who dropped in periodically, like an uncle or a repairman. That wasn't the kind of marriage I wanted, and it certainly wasn't how I wanted to raise a child. I wanted us both involved."

"It would have gotten better. I only had another six months of hell and then it would have eased up. If you had trusted—"

"I still don't see how it would have been any different after you finished the program. You liked being at the hospital. You complained about everything when you were home. As much as I wanted you to be at home, a part of me dreaded it."

"My God, Jessie, did you ever really love me? Why the hell did you marry me?"

Her throat hurt from holding back the tears, then her chest tightened, the pressure of the emotions crushing her lungs. She gathered herself to scream or lash out physically, anything to relieve the agony. Instead, for once, she let her tears stream down her face. She told him the truth that she'd always hidden from herself. "I married you because I loved you more than I loved anything else in this world, including myself."

"You had a funny way of showing it," he said, his voice less angry but cold. He got up and walked into the house.

Jessie wanted to run after him and shake him until he understood that he'd made her divorce him. He'd walked out first, emotionally. She'd had to leave or lose herself. She looked deep inside and was bare-butt naked honest with herself. What did she want him to say? That he was sorry for not loving her enough to give up his own dreams? When she'd filed for divorce, she'd wanted him to come crawling back to say that and more. The past three years *had* changed her. She'd had to rebuild herself from rodeo trick rider to therapist. That transformation had been painful and heart wrenching at times. She'd faced all of it without flinching. She wiped at her tears and followed Payson inside.

When she stepped through the sliding door, he clicked off the TV. Another tear made its slow way down her cheek as she stood in front of him. She wanted to look in his eyes as they talked. He held out his hand. She shattered, more tears wetting her face as she sank beside him on the couch. His arms enclosed her and his hands held her softly but with a strength that anchored her. That's what she'd searched for, then and now—the freedom to go her own direction, knowing that he was there to hold her when she shattered into a million pieces, to catch her when she fell.

"Payson," she whispered.

"Shh," he said. "It's been a tough day. We can't change the past. I know that, but we can change how we view it. Don't you think we started that tonight?"

Jessie didn't want to talk anymore, so she sat quietly, the tears on her cheeks drying but her eyes still damp. When she finally felt him shifting, she didn't want to move.

"Let's get comfortable," he said softly. His hands and fingers found the tightness in her neck and shoulders as he stretched out and pulled her down beside him. She draped herself over him, her face comfortably nestled into the curve of his neck where she could feel his warmth and smell the familiar spice of him. He let his breath out on a deep sigh, settling her more firmly against him.

"Thank you," she mumbled, and her brain sluggishly considered shifting away, standing up and going to bed on her own. Talking about Violet and those days after the miscarriage had made her unsteady, craving his touch. It'd been his love—always—that had kept her strong. Strong until the never-ending grind of trying to mesh their clashing schedules, their different dreams, their different lives had made her forget that his love was a support, not just a heavy blanket. So she'd pushed him away because she thought standing on her own, being strong by being alone, would finally make her heart safe. Maybe she'd been wrong. Maybe she should have turned to him, rather than away.

His arms tightened just a fraction more. She didn't pull back. She clasped him more closely to her, as she would a hurting child, a frightened pony or her best friend. Payson wasn't any of those, but they both needed the human touch for right now. Tomorrow she'd struggle back up onto her own two feet.

Chapter Nine

Payson woke, the warm weight of Jessie wrapped around him. He should get up and go to his very solitary bed, leaving her the couch. That would be the gentlemanly thing to do.

She mumbled in her sleep, and he held her tightly against him, stroking her hair. The familiar feel of her against him took him right back to their life together— the freedom and joy he'd felt each time they'd made love. Their teenage passion had matured during the marriage into something that, while intense and all consuming, had a softer side. He wasn't sure he'd ever find that again. He clutched her to him, wanting to hold on to that feeling.

Then, with an odd sensation that was somewhere between dreaming and waking, he didn't question that he was back in their old apartment as he watched *his* Jessie walk across the bedroom with that rolling-hipped stroll that made him want her right then and right there. She smiled. She knew the effect her cowgirl walk had on him. He didn't care. He wanted her to know what she did to him because he knew from the deep green of her eyes that she felt the same heat. He reached out for her, and she stepped into the loose circle of his arms, magnificently naked. With her height and with him sitting, his face rested comfortably in the valley of her breasts as her hand stroked his hair. He sighed, his breath moved across her chest. Her nipples peaked. He smiled. He liked watching her respond so quickly and thoroughly to his touch.

She moved closer, her hands tangling in his hair as she let out a breathy sigh. His hands explored the long length of her back, settling to where it curved into the strong roundness of her buttocks. He leaned back on the bed and she followed him down. Her body covered his with her heat and yielding softness.

"Payson," dream Jessie whispered. "Stop fooling around. I need you."

Her impatience made him want to laugh, to take her hard and fast. Not this time, though. He'd stretch out their loving so he could feel the play of muscle under her skin and watch that skin pebble where he touched it. The physician in him knew the detailed reasons for the changes, but the lover enjoyed that he could make the strong Jessie a pliable puddle with his fingers and tongue. That's what he wanted to do now. He wanted to take control. In bed, Jessie never complained that he was the one calling the shots. He lifted her away from him so he could roll her under him. He heard her squeak and then he was free-falling.

He wasn't dreaming now as they hit the floor with a solid thump, Payson on top of Jessie. He lay for a moment, stunned. He wanted to move. He knew he should, but the sensation of Jessie under him was so sweet.

"I'm sorry," he whispered in her ear, giving himself more time. "Are you okay?" He moved his hands down her body, stroking her just a little to assure himself this was real.

JESSIE TRIED TO PUSH away sleep. Her sluggish brain told her that she and Payson had fallen from the sofa. Her arms—not fully connected to her brain—wrapped around him. She stroked them down his back as she always did after they made love.

With every inch of their bodies touching, her nerves pulsed, centering on the spot where he nestled between her thighs. She moved just a little to ease the ache. Payson groaned deep in his chest. The primal sound vibrated through her.

Remember the divorce, she told herself. *Remember the pain.*

Payson's familiar and skilled hands moved under her shirt and along her sides to a spot just above the band of her jeans. Her traitorous body arched into the caress. "Payson," Jessie said softly, but he nuzzled her neck, and she didn't know what she'd meant to say, except maybe, *Don't stop.* Her own hands slid under his shirt, sinking into his firm back muscles. She sealed her mouth to his, reveling in his taste and the weight of him.

Then his hands were at her jeans, and she lifted so he could pull them down without breaking the kiss. Her hands fought with his to rid him of his pants and his briefs.

For one breathless moment, he hovered over her, his blue gaze locked on her, searching her face, and she gasped, "Payson, now, please."

He didn't look away as he plunged forward and she lifted up to meet him. For another second they stayed frozen, her body adjusting again to him. When he moved faster, more surely, she met his every thrust with an upward, triumphant move of her own hips.

Seconds, hours later, she flew apart, her back arching

and her body shuddering. Payson's low groan of satisfaction took her back up to the peak and she shuddered in the final complete surrender and triumph.

Jessie lay for a moment, breathing quickly and deeply, her body molding to Payson's in the barely wide-enough space between the couch and the coffee table. She didn't feel the roughness of the rug or the hardness of the floor, her body numbed by pleasure. Payson stirred, and she saw his mouth open. She snapped her eyes closed, blocking out whatever regrets he would voice. He remained quiet and shifted away. She stopped herself from yanking him back into the cocoon that included just the two of them, where the real world wasn't allowed to intrude.

When she heard him walking away and then back to her, she kept playing possum even as he tenderly placed a pillow under head and covered her with a blanket. She heard him sigh, and the next noise she heard was the shower running.

With him safely in the bathroom, she opened her eyes, sat up and gathered her clothing. She raced to the spare room. Oh, God, what had she done? She stood in the small room with its futon and bare walls, her clothes pressed against her stomach, frozen with indecision. Her gut told her to run as far as she could. But she had nowhere to run and no money to run with. She collapsed onto the futon. This had been a huge mistake. What had she been thinking about? Nothing but the pleasure of his touch. And neither of them had bothered with protection. Where was she in her cycle? Could they have made an even worse mistake? Could she already be pregnant? She counted again. They should be safe, but nature had a way of surprising you. For a fleeting second, Jessie really wanted nature to surprise her.

PAYSON LET THE hot water run over him, hoping the pounding spray would give him a jolt of inspiration. Instead, Jessie filled his mind. Finding her under him had been… It didn't matter what it had been, other than a mistake. He wasn't a teenager, and he should have had better control over himself. He had stopped being a walking bundle of hormones years ago, but not tonight. He'd even forgotten protection. What had he been thinking? How sweet and yielding she felt under him? Yeah, that was about it. His dream about Jessie had gotten mixed up with finding her pressed up against him in real life. Being half-asleep was no excuse. He'd known in that cold clinical part of his brain exactly what he'd been doing, which hadn't stopped him from wanting one little taste. That one nibble had led to another and another and… He turned off the shower and stood for a moment. No matter the consequences, they fit together as if they'd never been apart, her skin just as soft and her responses racing through him. It had been different, too, something deeper—less combustion and more slow burn. Later. He'd think about all of this later.

While he shaved, he laid out today's game plan. First, he'd tell Jessie he needed to spend the day at work, which wasn't a lie. And being in the quiet of the weekend hospital might help him figure out what this morning meant, besides the most satisfying sex—all right, the only sex—he'd had since their divorce. He also had to wrap his head around the idea that what they'd done this morning could result in a pregnancy. He leaned over to rinse his face so he couldn't see his grin at the thought of a baby.

HE DIDN'T HEAR or see Jessie when he finally came out of his room, and he resolved to give her space today. She was probably regretting what they'd done. Payson stood in front of the closed spare-room door, listening, he told himself, not putting off this first awkward…whatever. *Just knock on the door.*

"Jessie," he said as he knocked. He listened for a moment and knocked again.

Through the closed door, Jessie said, "Do you need something?"

"Just wanted to let you know that I'm going to the hospital."

A brief silence and the door opened, "Can you give me a ride to the ranch?"

Was the red on her neck whisker burn? "Forgot about your Scout," he said, dropping his gaze, which didn't keep him from taking in the scent of her.

"Are you ready now?"

"If you are," he said, wanting to get beyond this stiff politeness but not sure how. "I'll meet you by the Range Rover."

He didn't wait for her answer but moved quickly to get his keys. The thirty minutes out to the ranch would give them a chance to…what? Talk? They weren't so good at that. Or they hadn't been. Last night on the patio proved that they had changed. So today in the car did he say thanks for the incredible morning sex? Or did he just ask her what she wanted for dinner?

"THANKS FOR GIVING me a ride," Jessie said as he pulled onto Scottsdale Road from his place.

He nodded. "When do you need me to pick you up?"

Jessie kept her gaze glued to the rushing traffic. "I'll get a ride. When will you be back at the condo? It'll take me a couple of hours to take care of the stock and then

I need to…I guess I'll be out there most of the day. I should be back by dinnertime. Don't you still keep a key hidden under a rock? You always did that at our place."

He refused to be disappointed that she'd be gone all day, because that's what he had planned, too. "It's the rock to the left of the front door, with the black streak through it," he admitted. "You want me to do…I mean, *make* anything special for you tonight?"

"You don't have to cook for me." She glanced over at him, then went back to staring out the side window. "This morning shouldn't have happened."

She *did* want to talk about it. But what should he say? "It's understandable. Scientifically, we—"

"Really, that's the argument you're going with?" Now, she glared at him.

"I don't know what I was going to say," he blurted out. He gripped the steering wheel hard and kept his gaze glued to the white car in front of him. "I didn't ask you stay with me for *that*."

"Good to know, but it can't happen again. We're divorced. There has been a lot of water under that bridge."

Even when he had to tell his patients' parents bad news, he didn't feel as out of his element as he did now.

"We agree," she said. "We're only colleagues."

"That's right," he said, wondering if her voice sounded unsure.

"I won't be staying long, anyway. Spence is on the case. I'm sure he'll want to get you out of my clutches as fast as he can."

"He's doing this as a favor, and I don't think he dislikes you as much as you imagine." He looked over to see her shoulders hunch just a little.

"Thanks for calling him," she said quietly.

"You're welcome."

They lapsed into silence, and he turned on the radio. Obviously, they had completed their big talk. His cell rang, and he used voice commands to answer without looking at the caller.

"Dr. MacCormack here."

"Cut the crap. It's just me," Spence said with gruff impatience.

"Not had your coffee? I'm just taking—"

"Everything's closed up tight for the weekend, and we'll be lucky to get the judge to look at the papers on Monday."

"What do you mean?" Jessie cut in. "I need to get back in my house, and I have—"

"Jessie? Didn't know you were there. I'd say we'll be lucky to get anything more than a stop on the auction this week. But that doesn't mean you'll get back in the house."

"She really does need to be able to get into her home," Payson said.

"She's staying with you. You have two bedrooms at your place and it's free. What's the problem?"

Payson scrambled for explanation about why it *was* a problem and keeping what happened private.

"Oh, shi…you slept together, didn't you?" Spence asked, obviously thinking he already knew the answer.

"That's none of your business," Payson said to cover Jessie's gasp. "Keep us apprised of your progress." Payson clicked off the phone with a button on his steering wheel.

JESSIE KNEW IF never-off-his-phone Spence figured out that they'd slept together, everyone else would, too. She snuck a glance at Payson and their gazes locked, the tingle of awareness starting again. How did he do this to her? "It was a lucky guess," she finally said.

"Spence won't say anything to anyone."

"Are you ashamed of what we did?" she snapped. Of course he was ashamed. The morning should never have happened, and it didn't change anything between them.

"Not ashamed, but it wasn't my finest moment," he said quietly. "I didn't even protect you."

"I'm an adult. I can take care of myself." A classic Payson move—thinking that he had all of the cards and that put him in charge.

"I hadn't just been kicked out of my house."

"So you think I was so upset and pathetic that I was willing to take comfort anywhere?"

"That's not what I meant," he said, voice low and rough with frustration. "You always take what I say the wrong way. I know you're competent. I know you can handle yourself."

She held back for a moment, giving her brain a chance to catch up with her emotions. "I'm sorry," she said. "I shouldn't have jumped on what you said. It's not like… This is just so darned awkward."

He turned and smiled at her. She sucked in her breath as that shy grin went right to her heart, the way it always did. Just in time, she stopped herself from grinning back.

He reached out his hand to take hers as he left the highway to wind through the narrow roads to the ranch. "Awkward to say the least, but we lived through the at-home dye job."

The laugh burst from her before she could stifle it. He squeezed her hand as she said, "You mean when you turned my hair from Luscious Lemon Blond to greener than a leprechaun?"

"Good thing I'd learned all that chemistry."

"Hah! I know you called your mom's stylist, and she gave you the stuff for my hair."

"Busted," he said without heat.

She pulled her hand from his when she saw the turn-off to the ranch. Reality. They weren't a couple, and her biggest problem wasn't green hair. Her stomach dipped as she saw the tacked-up notices.

"Are you sure you'll be okay by yourself?" he asked without looking at her.

"Why wouldn't I be? I'm here by myself all of the time." She didn't stop herself from sounding belligerent.

"You have your cell, right?" he asked, holding lightly on to her arm when she opened the door. She nodded. "If you need anything, call me. Call someone."

"I've been on my own for three years." Hearing those words opened the raw place in her heart that hadn't completely healed since Violet. "Go save a life or something. I've got stalls to clean." She slammed out of the SUV to prove to herself that she could. What she and Payson had done this morning wasn't reality, it was just a memory of their past. Her reality, the only one she wanted, was Hope's Ride, helping children and standing on her own. She glanced over her shoulder. Payson sat there watching her. An involuntary and unwanted shiver ran from her stomach to her breasts as his gaze slid across her skin.

Chapter Ten

Pulling her ball cap firmly into place, Jessie readied herself for the morning's work, shoving Payson far away from her thoughts. From outside the barn, she heard a stomp and a kick, followed by the rattle of the chain on one of the stalls. She hurried into the darkened aisle, tracing the noise to Molly—of course.

Jessie reached in to pat the little animal. Molly backed away and bared her teeth, making Jessie laugh. She knew why the pony was out of sorts. There weren't any children around to spoil her with apples and whatever candy they had in their pockets. Jessie'd always imagined that when she and Payson had a child, their little one would learn to ride on Molly. While the pony could be a handful, she was always gentle when a new rider sat on her back. She seemed to know when she needed to stop her shenanigans.

Their child… Jessie's hand crept to her belly. Could she be pregnant? It was possible.

Another horse pushed his head over the half door and a whinny came from the far left. Back to work. The horses needed to be fed and watered. She gave Molly a final pat, avoiding the snapping teeth.

An hour later, the quiet of the barn had soothed Jessie

enough that she didn't mind when Lavonda interrupted her, insisting that she wanted to help after hearing an edited version of what had been going on at the ranch.

"I told you before. I miss the horses," Lavonda said firmly. "Even cleaning out the stalls. But you do Molly and Bull."

"It's a deal. Since you're here, let's turn them out for a little bit, run off some of that energy. I don't want them all full of sass and vinegar when the kids come back."

"So you'll be opening on Monday?" Lavonda asked as they got the buckets of feed organized for the horses.

"It all depends on the judge. Spence is working on that. I can't imagine we won't be back in full operation by Tuesday."

"What about after that? I'm your sister so I'm just going to ask about the money. Where are you getting that? You told me not to say anything to Mama and Daddy, but I have money from my severance…"

Jessie's gaze flashed up from the bucket of feed. She could not take money from her little sister. "I'll get more time once they know the hospital is involved."

"If you say so. And like I've told you, if you ever need help with fund-raisers or working with donors, I did all of that in my other life."

"But you said that you don't want to do that anymore. What *are* you going to do? Mama told me you haven't even applied for a job," Jessie said, feeling bad that she hadn't asked before.

"I'm taking my time to figure out what to do next. No need to sic Mama on me. I'm doing some freelance projects." Lavonda turned away with a bucket in each hand. She didn't want to talk about it obviously.

Hours passed as Jessie and Lavonda cared for the

animals, gave them a little time out of doors and then rounded them up again. They kept the conversation light.

The last animals to return to the barn were, of course, Bull and Molly. The two companions trotted around the paddock, resisting all of the sisters' tricks to herd them back into the barn. Jessie knew that if she could get Molly into the stall, Bull would follow.

"Darn it, Molly," Jessie yelled in frustration. "Get over here." The pony trotted serenely out of reach, kicking up her heels as she passed by.

"She's being a stinker," Lavonda said.

"Yeah. I'm even willing to bribe her, but I don't have any candy with me."

"Wait a second. I think I have something in my car." Lavonda raced off to her red Mini Cooper. The car was out of place on a working ranch, but if it held candy, Jessie thought it was about the most useful vehicle around.

Her sister held up a clear plastic bag of colorful candy. Jessie gave Molly a disgusted look as the pony stopped and stared at Lavonda. "You don't deserve one treat," she said, reaching for her halter. Molly raced off, only coming back when Lavonda put six gummy worms in her palm. Molly delicately lipped them into her mouth, calmly going into her stall while Jessie herded Bull in after her.

"Darn it, Molly," Jessie said when the pony kicked over the bucket of water. It would have to be refilled before they left. Jessie handed the bucket to Lavonda, who left the stall to fill it up. Jessie walked up to Molly, snatching her halter so she could talk with the pony eye to eye. "No more. You need to settle down. The kids won't be here for a few days." Molly tried to shake away. Jessie held firm. "I know. I'm not happy either, but it's just the way it is. They'll be back soon." Jessie felt her throat tighten. She leaned down to give Molly a hug just as the pony swung her head up. The thunk of thick equine skull against Jessie's chin made her see stars. She staggered back and Bull snorted, then sidled over, pinning her against the wall, shoulder first. "Oomph," Jessie said.

"Are you okay?" Lavonda called. "Bull, out of the way." The other woman pushed into the stall. Molly sniffed at Jessie, then chased Bull away.

"I'm fine," Jessie breathed. Her shoulder hurt where she'd nailed it on the metal hayrack on the wall. The impact had numbed her fingers, and her face ached from Molly's thump.

Lavonda ignored her words and helped her from the stall. After making sure the door was locked, she turned to Jessie. "How many fingers am I holding up?"

"You're a doctor, too?"

"That's what they always do on *Trauma ER*."

"I'm fine, just a couple of bruises. All in a day's work."

"I don't care if you're older than me. You need a keeper. I'm coming out tomorrow to help, too. Unless Payson's finally going to step up and help with the actual chores, instead of just filling out paperwork."

"He'd rather clean the bathroom with a toothbrush than come out here." Jessie stopped herself from going off on a lengthy tirade. "His schedule is full most of the time, and you know he's not a horse guy."

"What time tomorrow?"

"Seven a.m.?"

"Great. I'll bring the coffee." Lavonda stared at Jessie's chin. "It's already starting to bruise. You'd better get home and put ice on it."

"Home? This is home," Jessie said, the good mood disappearing.

"Figure of speech, and you'll be back here before you know it." Lavonda gave Jessie a little hug.

"Without Hope's Ride, I..." Jessie stopped talking and pulled away from Lavonda. She was the big sister and had to get ahold of herself. Boo-hooing about the situation wasn't going to get it solved. "We're all done here. Let's go."

The two walked to their cars together. "Thanks, worrywart," Jessie said, hopping into her pickup. "See you tomorrow."

It was a relief to get back to her truck because she didn't want to rely on Payson for rides. She watched her sister race down the dirt track, surprised by the speed of such a dinky car. Without Lavonda's help today, Jessie would still be cleaning stalls. When other volunteers had heard about the ranch's troubles, they'd said that they would do whatever she needed. She hadn't wanted to believe it, but after the third call today, Lavonda had pointed out to her that the others really did want to help. They weren't just being polite. Her sister might actually be right.

As Payson pulled into the garage, he was secretly pleased that he wouldn't be walking into an empty condo. During their marriage, he'd savored the times Jessie was there when he came home—maybe because she was on the road so much. He loved when the house was bright with lights and the air inside scented with Jessie—hay, mesquite and Ivory soap. Home. He shook his head to rid himself of the nostalgia.

"Jessie," he said as he walked in. She didn't answer.

He went down the short hall to the spare room. The door was closed, so he knocked.

"Come in," she said.

"I know it's early, but I wondered if you…" He stopped when he saw that she held a plate with just a lone crust of bread. "You already ate."

"You don't mind, do you? There were cold cuts in the fridge."

"You're my guest," he said. "*Mi casa es su casa.* I was going to suggest going out for something to eat, but that's okay."

"Sorry. I didn't know."

"Everything fine at the ranch?" he asked.

Jessie turned her head, wincing and exposing a dark purple bruise on her face.

"What the hell happened to you?" he asked, rushing to her. He reached out his hand to hold her face steady, so he could see the damage she'd done this time. "Did you lose consciousness? Do you have a headache? Double vision?" She tried to shake her head away. He held her firmly. "How many fingers?"

"Would you stop," she said, wrenching away and immediately stopping to hold her shoulder still. "Molly and I bumped heads and I hit the hayrack. It's nothing."

"And, of course, you were by yourself. What would have happened if you'd passed out? No one would have found you for hours."

She glared at him and said, "Actually, Lavonda showed up to help."

Seeing her hurt…again…made him a little crazy. Had he ever responded the way he planned to when it involved Jessie? He stepped back and said, "I'll get you an ice pack for your shoulder. It won't help the bruise on your chin."

"My chin's no worse than when one of the kids accidently hits me. The shoulder's pretty tender. That darned hayrack hit right on my shoulder blade."

"Why don't you go to the living room. The TV in there is a lot bigger." She nodded her head. She'd taken his pathetic olive branch.

As he got the ice pack ready, Jessie sidled past him and dropped her dirty dishes in the kitchen sink. Then she hurried to the living room couch, channel surfing until she found a rodeo, which, no matter the time of day, she had a knack for ferretting out. He made himself relax. She wasn't trying to annoy him. She genuinely loved the rodeo. He held out the bag of ice, wrapped in a dish towel. She took it and wiggled until she had it between her back and the couch.

"Would you like to join me for a beer or a glass of wine? It *is* Saturday night."

"A beer would be great," she said. The TV went to commercial, and Jessie called into the kitchen, "What did you do today?"

"Went into the hospital to do paperwork. Everyone keeps talking about the paperless office, but I don't see it," he tried to joke.

"I'm always amazed how many forms I have to fill out every time I accept a new student."

Payson relaxed. Maybe they could have a conversation just like a couple of old friends. He looked down at her. Her hair had fallen from her ponytail and her T-shirt was half in and half out of her jeans. She looked like what she was—a cowgirl at the end of a long day of work. She looked like a woman he wanted to take to bed. Crap. That was definitely not what he wanted to do. She reached out to take the bottle from him and their fingers touched. Desire shot through him.

"FOR GOODNESS' SAKE," Jessie said, grabbing the bottle after Payson fumbled it.

He spun away and a second later she heard him open the fridge. Drawers opened and closed, and he asked with little enthusiasm, "So the horses were all okay?"

"I'm sure they think they're on vacation. Molly was extra cranky, though. She misses being spoiled by the kids," Jessie said. She made a few more comments about the ranch, her attention split between the rodeo on TV and Payson. He sat beside her, propping his feet on the coffee table to make a place on his lap for the thick sandwich resting on a paper towel. She wiggled on the couch to get the numbing cold in just the right spot.

"Do you need more ice?" Payson asked, reaching over to help her adjust the packet.

His warm hand sharply contrasted with the ice. She'd felt the light caress of his fingers just before his whole arm jerked away from her. "I'm good," she said, her voice tight, her skin sensitive.

"I can come out tomorrow and help," he said, picking up the sandwich and immediately putting it down. "After rounds, I'm free for the rest of the day. It would get me out of cleaning up around here."

Safe topic. Good. "You think cleaning out stalls would be better than running a vacuum?"

"I really hate to vacuum," Payson said with a nearly natural grin.

"No, you don't," she said and without thinking added,

"I remember how you wanted all of the tracks in the carpet to go the same way. It took you forever to do a room."

"What can I say? I'm a detail man."

Which were the exact words he used when they made love and she thought he was going too slow. Heat flushed through her, pooling between her thighs. This was why she'd been in her room. Being together led to all kinds of innocent remarks and glances turning her into a hot and bothered cowgirl. She couldn't let anything like this morning happen again.

"I'm really beat," Jessie said abruptly, not looking at him. "I'd better get to bed."

"It's early," Payson said.

"You know us ranchers—up at the crack of dawn." She headed down the hall before he could say anything else. She turned on the small TV in the spare room, keeping the volume low. When she could no longer hear him moving around, she scurried to the hall bathroom for a quick shower. She needed to relax and wash away the memory of his touch.

Cleaned up, she lay down on the futon, listening to the hum of cars on the highway and the blare of a truck horn. She forced her eyes to close and immediately relived the morning on the floor with Payson. Memories from their marriage followed. Ones that, until the danged bank had kicked her out of her house, she had been doing a good job of forgetting. She turned onto her side facing the door. Had that been the creak of Payson's bed? Was he as restless as she was? Maybe none of this got to him. Except he'd pulled away from her on the couch as though he'd touched a hot pan. But, then again, she didn't know this Payson. She knew the old one. She had to remember that.

JESSIE AVOIDED PAYSON on Sunday morning by leaving for the ranch very early. Lavonda came by again to help, and, more importantly, she brought coffee and bagels slathered with cream cheese. Payson, of course, didn't show up later, and Jessie didn't care why. She reminded herself that he was in it for the title and cleaning stalls wouldn't get him there. On Monday morning, Jessie quietly left before sunrise. She told herself on the drive to the ranch that she'd get the chores done quickly, then she'd sit down in her office and start making calls to get financial help and find out when the hospital staff would be back. No one would fight as hard for Hope's Ride as she would. Spence could keep doing his legal thing, but she wouldn't leave the fate of her program in anyone else's hands.

With her course set, she got to cleaning the stalls. The usual sense of accomplishment from tidying up the barn and working with the horses lasted through the first three calls she made, including the one to the department head at the hospital, who told her that the stipend and the visits from staff were on hold. Stubbornness kept her on the phone. After the fifth please-call-back-later, Jessie wanted to throw the phone across the room. Instead, she forced herself to stroll outside and sit on one of the benches her brother had built. She closed her eyes and breathed in the dusty desert and slightly acrid scent of the manure pile. When Lavonda's cheery red Mini Cooper pulled up, Jessie decided her arrival was a good thing. Chatting with her sister would be a good distraction.

Jessie called, "All done this morning. Sorry you drove all the way out here."

"Oh." Lavonda sounded disappointed. "I knew I was late…can I come back and help this evening?"

"I've got it handled. You've already done so much."

Her sister frowned. "I want to, and I've barely done anything. You didn't even ask me for a place to stay." Lavonda paused and worked on a smile. "If you don't need me for the barn work today, at least let me help with the other stuff. You know, looking for donors, doing PR."

Jessie opened her mouth to protest but noticed how tense her sister's shoulders were. And Lavonda's eyes were suspiciously bright. Something was going on. Slowly, she said, "If you have the time to help with fundraising, I won't say no. You know how crappy I am at asking for any kind of help."

"It's a Leigh thing. I guess I got all of the asking genes from Mama's people."

Jessie, like her daddy and brother, sometimes took independence a little far, but she wasn't stupid. Lavonda had been great at her job and had been on half a dozen nonprofit boards, always asking for money. Plus Jessie'd come up with squat for a plan, other than calling people and trying to talk to them, which, in her desperation, might have been a little more like bullying.

Jessie took a deep breath and managed to smile as she said, "If you have ideas, I'd love to hear them." That hadn't been as hard as she imagined.

"Would you like to get some lunch? I could go over what I've been thinking about," Lavonda said. "I know you don't have volunteers helping with the fund-raising, and—"

"I'm horrible at asking for money...obviously, or I wouldn't be shut down."

"It's an acquired talent." Lavonda's smile made her face look much younger, like the little girl who had helped Jessie braid their ponies' manes.

"Good. Because I need to acquire it fast." Jessie's mood instantly lightened and the tightness in her stomach eased.

PAYSON HAD BEEN certain he would see Jessie before he left for work on Monday but that didn't happen. As usual, she was going it alone. Damn that woman.

Because so much of his schedule had been cleared to oversee Hope's Ride, he had the time to dig further into a plan to get Jessie's program reopened and solvent. Spence had the legalities under control, although another call to light a fire under his brother wouldn't hurt.

Payson had spoken with his financial guy about getting money for the program, which the man had advised against, even after Payson had explained thoroughly that the donation was an investment in his career, starting with becoming director of pediatrics. Next, he searched the hospital's internal network for grants and donation opportunities. Desert Valley's board was always looking for places to spend money and shine up the hospital's reputation as a "caring community health center." Payson couldn't imagine that the hospital wouldn't invest a little of its own money in Hope's Ride. He'd have Helen do more digging.

While Jessie might not be wrong about him liking to be in charge, he'd learned to delegate tasks or he'd never get to sleep. When he had a patient who needed help or he wanted to test out new equipment, he asked Helen. She had a knack for ferreting out obscure funding options.

The downside of money from the hospital was that the cash might take months to materialize. Long-term solution? Maybe. Jessie would ultimately have to decide on the grants because those sometimes came with strings. He didn't see strings and independent Jessie going together.

The best, quickest solution had him calling in favors and begging a couple of other doctors and family friends for cash. He didn't want to think about what he'd promised them for the money. By the end of this week, he was sure he'd not only have enough to bring Jessie's mortgage up-to-date but—this was key—there would be enough left over to get Jessie through the next few months until the hospital came through with its endorsement. Not only would that be good for Jessie, it would be good for his plans, too.

He barely acknowledged that he wanted Jessie on good financial footing in case she was pregnant…with his baby.

After pulling into his garage, Payson sat in his Range Rover, figuring out how he would present his plans. He'd just lay out the money situation in cold hard facts. She was an adult and she had a lot to lose. She'd listen, wouldn't she?

He found her in the kitchen. Her head snapped up, and he thought she looked guilty.

"I was leaving you a note," she said. "Lavonda promised that if I came to stay with her, she won't tell Mama and Daddy. I should have done that in the first place. I guess I was too stunned to think right."

"I spent my whole day saving Hope's Ride. You can at least stay until I tell you what I've worked out." He saw the change in her body.

"Excuse me," Jessie said slowly.

"I talked with the hospital. They would have found out sooner or later, and," he hurried on before she could cut in, "they are so convinced that the program is a winner that they've...umm...given you a grant. That's what they called it. A grant that doesn't have to be paid back, and there isn't even any paperwork because they're already working with you." It was a lie, and he watched her closely to see if she believed him.

"You talked to the hospital about all of this? I didn't ask you to."

"It was preemptive. They would have found out about the foreclosure," he said again. That was an argument Jessie might just accept. Why couldn't she be a reasonable human being? Anyone else would have been thrilled to learn that her financial problems were going to disappear and not ask too many questions.

"I told you that I could handle this myself and I am. Lavonda and I have come up with a plan," Jessie said. Her arms were crossed over her chest, her sage-green eyes narrowed.

"Jessie, the hospital's willing to give you this money. Take it before they change their minds." *Please take the money.* He worked to keep his expression pleasant and not give her a hint of his anger and fear.

"No. There'll be all kinds of strings attached, just like when I called you for help. No one ever gives you money free and clear. Lavonda and I have this covered. I can take care of this without more interference from the hospital."

"You need help right now. I got you the help."

"I didn't ask you to."

"I know, but don't be stupid." As soon as that was out of his mouth she gasped, and he immediately wanted to unsay it. "I mean, this is what you wanted, isn't it? To save Hope's Ride?"

"Thank you for letting me stay here," Jessie said and started to walk out.

"Wait. What if…" he began, but wasn't sure how he could say anything about the pregnancy. Instead, he went on, "I spent all day talking with—"

Jessie whipped around to face him and stepped right up to him, "I didn't ask you to spend a minute of your precious time. I am not taking the money."

"Saturday morning…what if…"

"That was a mistake. A big one. You don't need to worry. It's the wrong time," she said.

He didn't stop her when she walked out the door.

Chapter Eleven

"You should be the one they interview," Jessie said to Lavonda for the twentieth time in half an hour.

"It's your therapy program. You're the cowgirl, and there are people who will remember you from your trick-riding days. You are your own best spokesperson," Lavonda answered as she looked Jessie up and down.

They were just minutes from an interview with a Phoenix television news reporter and the kickoff to the press blitz that Lavonda had orchestrated. This was all possible because Spence had negotiated for more time from the mortgage company. It'd been like a Christmas miracle. She still owed the money, but she'd been given time—fingers crossed that it was enough.

Lavonda had convinced Jessie that the story of Hope's Ride was sure to get local media interest and had the potential to go national. Her sister's reasoning? Who could resist little kids and ponies fighting against big evil banks and hospitals? Jessie wasn't so sure that the hospital was "evil." Sure, they'd been slower than molasses in February and were withholding their funding till the money got sorted out, but the staff had been supportive. Still, Lavonda had convinced her that this strategy would get them what they needed. So Lavonda had passed along the information to bloggers and sent out a mass email to parents and volunteers with Hope's Ride asking them to share it with everyone they knew. All of that was how Jessie found herself standing in the late-afternoon Arizona sun, sweating and waiting.

Jessie pulled at her jeans again and wiped her palms along the sides of her legs while the cameraman got footage of the ranch, including the foreclosure notice, which had to stay until she'd deposited all she owed at the bank. Jessie, in a fringed and pearl-snapped shirt, would be taped leaning up against one of the corrals—"for that true Western look," the reporter explained. Lavonda insisted that Molly be in the shot, too. The pony waited more patiently than Jessie, stretching her muzzle through the slats of the fence to nibble at Jessie and beg for treats.

"Get her miked up, Len," the reporter said to the tall, thin camera guy. He got the microphone clipped to Jessie's shirt and hid the power pack at her back.

Her hands wouldn't stop trembling, and she wiped them on her jeans again. Lavonda now stood behind the camera guy, mimicking a big smile and pointing at Jessie.

Jessie pulled out her brightest rodeo smile, but she wondered from the odd look the reporter gave her if it was more like a grimace.

"Miss Jessie," Len, the camera man said. "Could you say something please? I need to test the volume."

"Something," Jessie said and laughed nervously. The camera man motioned for her to continue. "Hope's Ride is a—"

"That's good, ma'am. Thank you," he said, and nodded to the dark-haired reporter in heels and a Hillary Clinton pantsuit.

"Jessie, while I ask you questions," the woman said, "I want you talk to me and not look at the camera. Lavonda and I have gone over the situation, and I'll add the specifics in a voiceover later. From you, I want the flavor of the program. I want to understand why it's so important that you continue. Are you ready?"

Jessie wanted to shout *No.* "I'm ready," she said and blew out a nervous breath. This wasn't any different than performing in the rodeo, except it smelled better.

The reporter's gaze slid from Jessie and locked on the camera. She asked, "Jessie, you began Hope's Ride after you retired from the rodeo. Since then you've helped a number of children with disabilities or injuries. Can you tell me what is so special about these youngsters?"

After another deep breath Jessie said in a wavering voice, "Each child has touched my heart. Every one of them is working to overcome so much. They're so brave and uncomplaining. I am amazed every day."

"I understand that the riding provides physical rehabilitation for the children, but is there an emotional and psychological component, as well?"

"Yes," Jessie said, feeling calmer as she stared into the reporter's dark eyes. She only needed to convince this one woman of the near miracles that Hope's Ride performed. "The horses don't laugh at the children, and they don't care if the kids don't walk right or talk right. The horses give them kisses or gentle nudges because they are happy to see them. That sort of unconditional acceptance is essential. Then there is the fact that these children are in control of something so large. The horses listen to them, follow their instructions. The children feel so powerful after that. How can that not make them feel important and strong?"

Jessie relaxed another notch and talked about the children whose parents had given permission for their cases to be featured. "Alex," Jessie said and smiled. "He's a very brave little guy. He has a genetic disease that has led to a number of surgeries and put him physically behind other children his age. After starting at Hope's Ride, he began working harder at his traditional therapy and has come right out of his shell. He's doing better at school and his mother is so happy with his attitude. Even I've been amazed by Alex's progress," Jessie said. She was going to go on when a tug on her jeans pulled her to the fence. She automatically pushed Molly away.

"Who's that trying to get your attention?" the reporter asked.

"This is Molly," Jessie said, turning so the pony was visible. The camera man moved forward. "She's probably Alex's favorite animal at Hope's Ride. She was my pony, so she's got a little age to her. The children spoil her. Right now, she's really missing them."

"So other children like her, too? Do they ride her? How do they spoil her?"

"Molly's role is more a shepherd. She usually keeps the children gathered together and lets them groom her… and give her treats like apples and gummy worms," Jessie said and put her hand out to give Molly a pat. The pony laid her head on the railing. "Since I've had to close Hope's Ride, she follows me around as I clean stalls and then walks to the gate looking for the cars. She'll stand there for an hour or more. Then she shuffles back to her stall with her head down. While I was on the rodeo circuit, Molly was perfectly happy to stay behind and hang out with her horse friends. Once I started introducing her to the children at Hope's Ride, it's like she's found a whole new purpose. She takes her job very seriously. I don't know how she does it, but when a child is frightened or sad, she just knows. She'll go over and give them kisses." Jessie added without thinking, "Come closer. She'll give you one."

The reporter looked taken aback and totally uninterested in getting any closer to Molly. "It would be better if she demonstrated on you," the reporter said.

"Go on," the guy behind the camera said. "It'll be a great shot, Cassandra."

Jessie urged the well-dressed woman over, and Molly stamped her little hooves, kicking up a cloud of dust.

"Are you sure she's not going to bite me?" Cassandra asked.

"She just wants you to hurry up," Jessie soothed.

"Len, get the shot framed because I'm not doing this again," the woman said and took the final step toward Molly. The pony stretched farther over the railing and smacked her lips.

"Lean down," Jessie said. "She wants to kiss your cheek."

The reporter sucked in a breath and bent over, placing her face within easy reach of Molly. The pony sniffed delicately, then nibbled the woman's hair before pressing her muzzle firmly to Cassandra's cheek. "Oh," the reporter said, her voice hushed with surprise and pleasure. "She's so soft." Cassandra remained hunched over another moment or two and she reached out to hug the pony. When she finally stood back, Molly shook her head up and down, whinnied and ran around the corral two or three times to the delighted laughter of the reporter and cameraman.

Cassandra didn't move from the fence. When Molly came up again and tugged on her suit jacket, the reporter laughed and petted the pony. "It's obvious she loves people, isn't it?"

"Actually, all of the horses love people. They enjoy the work and the interaction with the students. They seem to know that their cargo is precious and fragile. Even when the students are brushing them, they behave."

"Do the young people do all of the grooming and care of the horses?"

"They do what they are able to because I tell them that cowboys and cowgirls always care for their mounts. We expect our students to perform the same chores that any young person learning to ride would, taking into account their limitations but pushing them to do more than they think they can. It's all part of the process of showing them that they can do anything."

"It must be extraordinary to see the changes in your students, their growth."

"It makes getting up before dawn every day and worrying every minute how to pay the bills worth it."

Cassandra gestured to the ranch. "And without help, you won't be able to get the program running again and keep it going, isn't that right?"

Even though she and Lavonda had discussed this part of the interview, it was still hard for her to ask for the help that she needed. *It's for the kids like Alex*, she told herself. In her mind, she could see his dear little face. She'd do anything for him, even beg for the money.

"I am working now to keep the bank and mortgage company from closing us down. We need to make up missed payments before it goes to a foreclosure auction. If the ranch is sold, the horses will have to find new homes, too. Most were adopted from other people or from rescue organizations. You've met Molly—I'm not sure what I'll do with her if I don't have the ranch.

"To keep the program viable, we've been working on receiving an endorsement from Desert Valley Hospital, which would have boosted the number of students whose fees would support the day-to-day operations, allowing us to raise money specifically to pay off the mortgage so we're not in this position again."

Jessie took a breath. She'd said it right, just the way she and Lavonda had planned. "A team of professionals from Desert Valley were here for a month before the shutdown forced them to delay their report. Without the report, the hospital's support may not come through."

"So, it sounds like you're hoping the Phoenix community will help you keep Hope's Ride open?"

"That's what we're hoping," Jessie said, and smiled. "We can't wait for Desert Valley to help these children. Hope's Ride is…I mean was…helping these very special and brave kids do things that they and their parents thought they'd never be able to do. It might sound… hokey…but we saw miracles every day. I guess, now, we're hoping for a miracle for Hope's Ride."

The silence made Jessie glance at her sister to make sure that she hadn't messed up. Lavonda's eyes were bright, but she was smiling.

"Perfect," said Cassandra. "We'll definitely end the piece with that. Len, get a little more B roll, then we're on our way." The reporter turned to Jessie, "Thank you. The interview was great. We'll do what we can. With all of the need in the community, I can't say what help you may get, but our viewers have been generous in the past."

"Anything would be a help. If we'd just had the hospital's endorsement, we would have been okay. Not rolling in money but able to pay all of the bills."

The reporter and cameraman thanked Jessie again and even went over to give the forlorn Molly a pat. The pony perked up and showed off again by galloping around and kicking up her heels. Everyone laughed. Molly looked over her shoulder, and Jessie was pretty sure she gave them a grin.

"It WENT BETTER than I thought it would," Lavonda said. "Molly is a real ham, isn't she? Was she like that when we were kids?"

Jessie watched her sister ruffle the pony's mane and said, "She was. You really think this will work?"

"It's kids and poor defenseless animals. People will definitely want to help. We have everything set up to take the donations. I still have feelers out to other media. We could get even more coverage. Everything will be fine. Let's change, finish up the stalls and then get lunch," Lavonda said, moving Jessie to the barns.

The women worked at the ranch for the rest of the day. Jessie called Spence again about getting into her house, but he'd had no luck. She would stay with Lavonda for another night.

They were both disappointed to find out the news story would not appear until the next day. A tiny part of Jessie was relieved that she could put off telling her parents and brother about the problems for a little longer. Lavonda put a good spin on it, though, telling Jessie the delay meant that the story was going to be more in-depth and longer. Two days later, Jessie was ready to go to the station and put the tape on air herself. After a call to Cassandra, Lavonda told Jessie the piece would run at the top of the five o'clock news—a good placement. The reporter said her station manager was going to offer the tape to other affiliates and the national network.

"If this thing goes national," Lavonda said as they sat in front of the TV and waited for the segment, "you won't need to worry about getting the hospital's support, or that Mama and Daddy will try to help out. You will have more than enough to keep Hope's Ride going."

"I just need enough to get the bank to leave me alone and call off the Humane League," Jessie said. She didn't want to imagine anything more. It would be all the more disappointing if the story didn't get national attention.

"Have you talked with Payson? Does he know about the story?"

"No," Jessie said shortly. She'd dreamed of them together again last night.

"You should tell him. I've known him long enough to know that he doesn't like to be blind-sided," Lavonda said.

"I'll text him," Jessie lied, refusing to look at her sister or think how the piece might affect Payson's chances of getting his directorship, which was as important to him as Hope's Ride was to her. Instead, she focused on watching the broadcast, reminding herself that she hadn't said anything but the truth. How could that be a problem?

By the time the piece on Hope's Ride was done, Jessie had swiped at her tears repeatedly. The reporter had done an amazing job capturing the essence of the program. She'd not only interviewed Jessie but also Alex, his mother and a number of other clients. The part of the broadcast where the president of the hospital refused to speak about the endorsement, hurrying away from the reporter, worried Jessie a little.

"That was perfect," Lavonda said. "You don't need to worry. You'll get more than enough to reopen the ranch."

Fifteen minutes after the broadcast, Jessie's parents called and could barely speak because they were so proud of her—and mad at her. They chided her for not calling them. They were only appeased because she had asked Lavonda for help. Her brother left a message and told her that she should've called him, too.

Lavonda's phone rang, but it wasn't a donation. Instead, a volunteer with the Humane League was calling to tell Jessie she needed to stop exploiting Molly. The next two calls were from animal rights activists who hated rodeos and complained loudly of Jessie's former involvement.

"What the heck?" Lavonda said at her phone. "That woman said that making Molly kiss Cassandra was cruel and unusual punishment. What is wrong with people? Why aren't they donating? Let me check the website. It probably crashed from all of the traffic."

Jessie knew what Lavonda would find. People didn't care. No, that wasn't fair. They cared, but there was so much in the world to care about. And she certainly wasn't surprised—or hurt—that she hadn't heard from Payson.

Two days later only one hundred dollars in donations had come in. She and Lavonda were getting dinner ready and not talking about the failure of the strategy when Jessie's phone buzzed in her pocket. She pulled it out and saw an unfamiliar number. She answered anyway.

"*Good Morning USA* here. We'd like to interview you live. Saw the Phoenix piece. The local affiliate will send a crew to the ranch at six a.m."

"Sure," Jessie said, stumbling over her words. "Six a.m. at the ranch."

"Perfect. Make sure the pony is there."

The phone went dead.

"What?" Lavonda asked as Jessie stood looking at her phone.

"*Good Morning USA.*" She stopped talking because her heart pounded so hard she was pretty sure she was having a heart attack.

"That was them on the phone?"

Jessie nodded because she couldn't talk. Lavonda punched the air. "We did it." Lavonda grabbed Jessie and hugged her hard.

Getting on national TV had been Lavonda's goal. Jessie never believed it would happen, and now it was and already her stomach was in knots. How many hours until she and Molly had to be on TV? Not enough. Did she need a manicure? Had she ever even had a manicure? What about makeup? She might have some in the back of a drawer but all of that was locked up in her house.

"Jessie," Lavonda said loudly and inches from her face. "Breathe. It will be fine. Give me the number and I'll confirm the details. This is what we wanted. This will save Hope's Ride. You can do it. Think of Alex and all of the other kids."

Her sister had it right. Jessie had to pull it together. If being on TV again could save her dream, then she would do it. But for cripes' sake, she just wanted to ride horses and help kids. That was all she had ever wanted—to be with her horses, her kids and…Payson. And two out of three wasn't bad.

"Go drink a glass of water or something," Lavonda said. "You still look like you're going to pass out. Remember, this is all good."

Chapter Twelve

As she opened the fridge, Jessie heard her phone play "Cotton-Eyed Joe" and her heart stopped. That was Payson. Why was he calling now? Hope's Ride had been on TV days ago. Maybe Lavonda had been right and she should have told him ahead of time. She caught his call just before it went to voice mail.

"Hello, Payson."

Silence, then a very hesitant and un-Payson like voice said, "Oh. Umm. I didn't think you were going to pick up."

She managed to stop herself from babbling like a teen.

"I just wanted to say congratulations," he said as another silence stretched out. "I heard you were on the news."

"We're going to be on *Good Morning USA* tomorrow," she blurted.

"That's fantastic," Payson said, but his enthusiasm sounded forced.

"Lavonda is sure that national exposure will get us the donations we need," Jessie said, not so sure after the lack of support with the local coverage. "Then I won't need to worry about when the hospital gives me its stamp of approval and it's good I didn't take that money you talked about. I'm sure it had all kinds of strings attached."

"I guess you owe me a steak dinner since you'll be world famous," he joked badly. "Just be careful about what you say."

"Lavonda and I rehearsed everything."

"I'm just giving you a heads up that the hospital is... image is important."

"They're the ones who won't be interviewed," Jessie answered hotly.

"I'm sure you've had one of your long days. I shouldn't have said anything."

"Stop treating me like a child."

"Jeez. I just called to congratulate you. Can't we even have a civil conversation?"

Jessie paced the apartment's galley kitchen. "I'm not apologizing." Even as the words came out, she knew she sounded like a pouty toddler. How did he so quickly reduce her to a witch with a B? "Let me start over." She stopped moving and said with every ounce of politeness she could muster. "Thank you for the call, Payson."

"You're welcome, and can I give you some advice about the hospital?"

"Yes, thank you." Maybe just saying the polite words would make her feel less cranky. Without that wall of hostility, though, would she start to feel that connection they'd had *that* morning?

"I know that working with Desert Valley has been a challenge for you with the paperwork and then withdrawing the staff. They're really just a big company, so it would be best if you could talk about the positive parts of the relationship and *not* about the problems you've had."

"Are you telling me to lie?"

"Jessie, if you repeat any of this, I'll be in big trouble," he said. "I got called into a meeting today. They're seriously considering pulling their support for the program's endorsement after watching the piece from local station."

"What?"

"Those of us working with you are trying to change their minds."

"That's blackmail. I just told the truth, and it wasn't even that bad. It's not like I said they were torturing kittens and starving puppies."

He blew out a long breath. "Jessie, you don't understand. All of the hospital's employees—even the doctors—are forbidden to say anything about the hospital. People have been fired for saying that Desert Valley makes them work long hours or that the cafeteria food is bland."

"So, if I say anything other than they are the best, I'll lose them as a supporter?"

"I'm not telling you what to do but…we're talking about Hope's Ride's future and possibly my career, too."

Jessie didn't know how to respond. Was he saying that what she'd said on TV could get him fired?

"Jessie? You still there? Just tell me where you're taping the national piece and I'll be there."

"You don't need to be there to make sure I don't mess this up. I understand what's at stake. Hope's Ride is—"

"Yours," he finished. "You've made that clear to me and everyone else—"

"I'm not going to cut off my nose to spite my face. *I'll* figure something out."

"If you just tell me where you're taping, I'll be there and we can practice," he said again, with more urgency.

The silence stretched out until Jessie finally said, "My family—Lavonda—will be with me. I don't plan to make trouble for Hope's Ride or you."

"I don't think you'd blame me for being a little controlling in this kind of situation. Plus, I've been dealing with the hospital administration for years. I understand how they think."

"I know, and I know how important your promotion and that new title are to you," Jessie said very, very quietly. More silence followed.

"I want to be there, Jessie, please," he finally said.

Maybe he should be there. It was his career, too. What he did for the children was just as important, even if he was doing it all for a stupid title. She stopped that line of thought. That was mean. She shouldn't belittle what he cared about. "I'm going on the air at six a.m. tomorrow. We're filming at the ranch. Lord help us all, but they want to have Molly on national TV." She tried to laugh.

"Thank you," he said quietly. "Good night, Jessie." She thought she heard him mutter "My stubborn cowgirl" before the phone went dead.

PAYSON CHECKED HIS phone as he got into his Range Rover before the sun even came up. He'd have just enough time to stop for coffee and make it to the ranch to discuss the interview with Jessie. His heart raced as he imagined what could go wrong. He'd heard from Helen, who'd heard from another woman at the hospital that the administration had convened an emergency meeting to address the "issue."

He drove on autopilot to the coffee shop, mulling over what Jessie might say to appease the hospital. Would she even consider it? What if she decided she didn't need him or the hospital? After she'd turned down their money, he'd had to backtrack and return everything. Maybe the TV interview didn't matter. Could anything she said today make a difference, or had the administration already seen this as damage done? Would they jettison the entire program, and Payson along with it for bringing Hope's Ride to them in the first place? He wished the coffee shop sold something stronger. Should he call his brother now, so he could get down here and make sure none of them got any deeper into the weeds? Probably too late. Or too early. The sun hadn't even cracked the horizon. He'd give him a call anyway and hope that Spence actually answered the phone.

Why hadn't he called Spence last night after talking with Jessie and finding out about the taping? Because all he'd been able to focus on was that he'd get to see Jessie.

IN THE GREEN-WHITE glow of the barn light, Payson watched Jessie stroll to the corral. His heart stuttered, then he firmly told himself that his career depended on what happened in the next few hours. *Concentrate on that, Payson Robert MacCormack.*

"Jessie," he raised his voice to catch her attention. "I got you fuel." He held up the cup.

Her head whipped around but her face stayed in shadow. "Come on. There's a ton to do. I've got to get Molly groomed and…come on," she said again. Obviously, he hadn't been moving fast enough.

He hurried to reach her. For a moment, he balked at being ordered around. Then he remembered what was riding on this morning's broadcast. "Maybe we should just cancel." Why hadn't he suggested that before? Because when it came to anything involving Jessie, his brain didn't work at full capacity. He might not be completely convinced of the measurable outcomes at Hope's Ride, like increased flexibility and strength, but he'd certainly come to believe that the psychological and emotional impact of the program had value for children like Alex.

"You're joking, right? I'm going to assume you're joking," she said with a squinty-eyed glare. "Fill this bucket with water, then we'll talk."

Twenty minutes later, he knew with certainty that they were all in trouble. Deep, can't-dig-your-way-out trouble. He shouldn't have been surprised. Jessie found a goal and got there on her own, never asking for help. That sometimes meant steamrollering over other people, including the hospital, based on what she said had been broadcast.

"I have the right to my opinion, and it's not like I lied."

"I know," he said, trying to slow down his heart and wondering if he had antacids somewhere in the SUV to calm his churning stomach.

"I worked on what to say. It's good."

"Going it alone again?" he asked and immediately wanted to kick his own butt. Jessie wasn't going it alone. She'd accepted his help and before that Lavonda's. He had to remember that she wasn't the Jessie he remembered, except in the most important ways—her bravery, her loyalty and her huge heart. "So what are you going to say?"

She shrugged tightly. "I'm not going to say anything if Molly doesn't get gummy worms and refuses to cooperate. I ran out. Could you go to the Min-It Mart and get them? You can be there and back in plenty of time."

He caught and held her sage-green gaze. Could he trust her? This was his career, his future. It was hers, too. Oh, God, if he hadn't been able to show her how much he cared, loved her while they were married, could he do it now? Would that heal the hole in his heart? He took the leap. "I trust you." He saw her stiff shoulders loosen and a smile—the real kind—curve her lips. The knot in his stomach loosened. "But I don't trust that pony, so I'll be getting a *big* bag of gummy worms."

"Payson," she said and gathered herself before she went on. "I'm not doing these interviews to hurt you. You know that, right? It's just that Hope's Ride…the children…damn…it's too early…I haven't had enough—" She stopped when Molly's solid head connected and made her stumble. Payson reached out to steady her. In seconds she was in his arms, cradled against him, her long length soothing him as much as exciting him with her strong curves.

He held her, not sure if there was anything he could say that would make either of them feel better. He softly kissed her temple, taking in her clean scent and finding a little more stability. "We fixed your hair, we can fix this." He heard a small puff of her laughter.

"That was much worse," she said, her face still buried in the side of his neck.

"Much worse," he agreed. They were silent for long seconds and her warmth and vitality slowly seeped into him, steadying his heartbeat, calming his mind. "So what are we going to do this time? I don't think my mother's stylist can help out."

Jessie gasped out a laugh and then her mouth was on his. He could taste desperation and something else. Then he didn't care because her arms tightened around him and he opened his mouth to her. He heard her sigh of pleasure as her tongue found his and her hands kneaded his shoulders. He pulled her closer by the full, round muscles of her buttocks. Once again their hips aligned perfectly and blood rushed to his groin. He groaned, or was that Jessie?

"Hey, you two, do I need to get the hose?" Lavonda asked.

They broke apart like a couple of teens caught making out in the back of Daddy's car. Payson looked at the ground as he gathered his thoughts. "Better go get those gummy worms," he mumbled. "I'll be back before the filming." Payson glanced at Jessie, whose fingers worried the snaps on her shirt. He saw the fullness of her lips from the kiss and wanted to take her in his arms again. He also saw that she was back to being the big bad cowgirl. In charge of the world and not needing him or anyone else. Was that the way it would always be?

JESSIE WATCHED PAYSON walk away, his shoulders tense. She knew that look.

"Hey," her sister said as she snapped her fingers in Jessie's face. "Focus, woman. We're going to be on national TV in T minus twenty."

"I know. I'm focused."

"Yeah, focused on gettin' some."

"I am not. Shut up." Had she just said that? She sound liked she was sixteen and fighting with her sister over whose shirt had the most fringe.

"Sorry. I'm nervous, too. What were you talking with him about?"

"The interview, of course."

"I bet they sent him to shut you up."

"I don't think so. It's his career."

"Just like it's the future of Hope's Ride and all of those kids."

"I know," Jessie said, glaring at her sister as Molly bumped her in sympathy.

"Payson and Desert Valley will be fine no matter what. They both can survive the fallout from any interview. And it was the hospital putting on the brakes that got us into this mess in the first place. But what about you and the kids? Hope's Ride is hanging on by a thread. To get people to pry open their purses, you need to tug a bit on their heart strings, but more importantly, you have to make it appear like they're fighting against a big soulless corporation and its minion…the minion being Payson."

"I thought you liked Payson."

"Like him? What does that have to do with anything?"

"My God, did they steal your soul before or after you got fired?"

"Very funny. They're playing hardball and so you need to, too. You can't get sentimental. This is war."

"I don't think it's—"

"Jessie, I worked in this world. They take no prisoners. It's win at all costs. Do you understand?" Lavonda's dark eyes were locked on Jessie. Her sister's petite frame vibrated with tension and intensity.

"I get it. I need to follow the script, throw the hospital…and Payson…under the bus to save Hope's Ride. I need to let everyone know that the big bad medical community only cares about making a lot of money, not about a program that really works, even if it may cost a little more than the conventional therapies. That's what I'm supposed to say, right?"

"You got it. Let's go over it one more time before Payson comes back with the gummy worms."

"No. I need to walk Molly, then we'll be ready."

Lavonda stared hard again and Jessie refused to look away. She would do what she needed to do, just like she'd always done.

Chapter Thirteen

"We understand that you've not had much cooperation from your local hospital, Desert Valley. Could you talk about that?" the anchor in New York asked Jessie.

Here it was. *The question.* She could see Payson, Spence and Lavonda just behind the camera. She could do this. She used her brightest rodeo smile and said, "Desert Valley has been very supportive of our efforts. They've been working closely with us to ensure the program is providing the children with the best care possible. Before we were forced to close by the bank and mortgage company, the team from Desert Valley had made great progress in quantifying the achievements. Sorry. In plain English what I mean is that without the hospital, Hope's Ride would not have been helping the children as well as we were. Once we get the money we need, then we'll be back to working with the hospital's team, and, most importantly, we'll all be back to helping the children."

Jessie kept her eyes on the monitor with the picture of the studio in New York. She could guess what Lavonda's expression was.

The remainder of the interview went well with more questions about the children and questions from viewers via Twitter about Molly. The whole interview took less than five minutes, but sweat dribbled down Jessie's back as if she'd done an entire trick-riding routine. She needed another shower and two pots of coffee to get back to normal after this workout.

EVERYONE WAS OVERLY polite as the film crew packed up and zipped away from the ranch. Jessie knew Lavonda was steaming. "Why did you ignore everything we rehearsed?" her sister asked flatly.

"I couldn't take the chance with Payson's career," Jessie said and felt Payson stir beside her.

"What about you and all of those children?"

"It didn't feel right putting Payson on the chopping block for Hope's Ride, plus it can't hurt to stay on the hospital's good side and to get their endorsement, right? Even you have to admit now that whether we blamed the hospital or the banks, Molly is what will get us the money. The tape they had of her even made me rethink the nasty names I called her yesterday when she stamped on my foot."

"That's not the point," Lavonda said. "We discussed a strategy and then you just did what you wanted. And why should you help *him*? What has he done but walk out on you? And, then, when you ask for help, he acts like he's master of the universe, ordering you around. And he's in it just for the title. You told me that."

"Wait a minute," Spence broke in as Jessie opened her mouth. "Without my brother, your sister's house would have been sold and her program would have been closed."

"Anything that Jessie has is because of her work. She doesn't need your family and their snooty help."

"I bet you'll hit up my parents," Spence said, leaning

close to Lavonda, "and all of their pals for money. Who else is going to—"

"Enough. The money doesn't matter right now," Payson cut in sharply. "Hope's Ride needs to have the chance to be evaluated, to prove its merits to the medical community. Making a difference for these children is what we all need to be focused on."

Jessie had to double-check that it was really Payson standing beside her. This was the first time he'd given Hope's Ride his full support. It wasn't a full-on endorsement, but it was more than he'd said before. They weren't out of the woods—or the cacti—but she relaxed a fraction, feeling hopeful. Her hand reached over to touch Payson's arm, to let him know how much she appreciated his support.

"What's going on between you two?" Spence asked, his tone sharp and demanding. "I know you slept—"

"We did not," Jessie snapped. She felt Payson freeze, so she squeezed his arm. "Payson is invested in Hope's Ride. After all, he'll only get to be director if the program works. Now, let's get the horses settled and ready for all of the donations." Jessie glanced at Payson and gave him a rodeo smile before she strode off.

What did they used to say on *The X-Files*? Plausible deniability. Neither Spence nor Lavonda knew anything for certain and it was going to stay that way. She didn't want her parents finding out. Like they would have if she'd been pregnant—but she wasn't, as she'd found out this morning. Time to focus on what was important in all of this. The interview was over. Payson's job should be safe and Hope's Ride would get the cash it needed. Until the money rolled in, she'd clean out stalls and check the corrals. Then she'd go get herself a big breakfast to celebrate.

THAT'S MY COWGIRL, Payson said to himself, watching her purposefully walk away from them. He smiled, then saw Lavonda's and Spence's faces and rearranged his lips into a firm line. "Some of us have jobs where someone would miss us if we didn't show up. See you later." He didn't slow when his brother called his name. He didn't want or need a third degree from Spencer MacCormack, Esquire, which was exactly how his brother acted when he got that certain gleam in his eye. He'd ask questions that Payson really didn't want to answer. Plus, he did have work at the hospital.

After doing rounds and consulting on two cases, Payson headed back to his office for a little bit of paperwork. He drank his tenth cup of coffee and choked down a dried-out ham sandwich as he typed, but his brain wouldn't stay focused. He kept seeing Jessie talking about the program this morning and standing up to her sister and his brother.

There had been that parting shot about him being director… Nothing was ever simple. Without her, his life had been going so well. He made it to work on time and could stay as late as he wanted. At home, his cereal stayed exactly where he'd put it. He never ran out of Dr Pepper or cheese for his quesadillas because he wrote it on a list he kept posted on the refrigerator.

He leaned back in his chair to stop the catalogue of pathetic reasons why his life was better without Jessie. That was superficial stuff. He knew that. He might be dense when it came to the emotional side of his life but not that dense. After that night at his condo and the next morning… No, not going there. Reliving that morning with her wouldn't help him finish the notes on the three patients he needed to discharge today. Plus, they were divorced. There was no undoing that.

His phone rang and he couldn't stop the sigh of relief at the interruption. "Yes, Helen," he said.

"I have the director of The Children's Hospital in Philadelphia on the line," she said, her voice overly professional.

"I don't have any patients there, do I?" He'd had other hospitals call when one of "his" kids showed up.

"Dr. Masterson said he would like to speak with you about Hope's Ride."

He hadn't realized that anyone beyond Desert Valley knew he worked with the program. Jessie certainly hadn't mentioned him. "Put him through."

The phone clicked without another comment from Helen, and the Philadelphia surgeon came on the line.

PAYSON TURNED OFF the Range Rover and looked around the spaces between the ranch buildings for Jessie. He couldn't believe that she'd be gone—it was only late afternoon. The woman worked harder than anyone else he knew, himself included. He got out of the SUV before he could think too hard about why he was here or what he would say. He looked down at his leather loafers as he walked across the dusty yard to the barn. He'd lived in Arizona his whole life and only owned one pair of cowboy boots, which he'd been given as a kid. Being bootless was a point of pride with him, probably a pointless point of pride. Jessie had teased him about it when they'd been young.

Focus, man. He'd laid out his tasks on the drive over: find Jessie, let her know that the hospital was content with the coverage, check on the donations, congratulate her again, go home, have a beer and decide what the call from Philadelphia meant.

"We're closed…" Jessie said as she met him just outside the barn. "Sorry. Didn't know you were coming out again. You didn't call."

He stopped his knee-jerk reaction to her belligerent tone and instead said, "If I caught you at a bad time, I can come back."

"It's fine. What do you need?"

He could tell she was working hard to maintain a smile. "Do you mind if we go inside? It'll be a little cooler." She stepped into the not-quite-so-hot barn where, damn it, he could see her even better. The jeans, the tight shirt, the light dew of sweat at her neck—all of it hit him in the gut. He wanted to taste the salt of a day spent working the ranch, and he wanted to run his hands along her sleek muscles. He looked away and said, "I came by to let you know that the hospital is fine with this morning's interview. Thank you. I don't—"

"I assume that means you won't lose your job and will get that fancy new title." She adjusted her stance, licked her lips and looked down. "If that's all, I've got to get back to work. I need to finish the feeding, and then I've got some phone calls to make."

"I'll help," he said on impulse. "Not with the calls, but I can put hay in the stalls and…stuff."

Her gazed focused on him and her eyes narrowed. "What do you want now?" she asked suspiciously.

"Nothing. Just to help. I've got the time."

She looked like she was going to say something else, but she shrugged and motioned for him to follow her. Her gait, not marred by her limp today, made her slim hips swing enticingly, and Payson reluctantly hurried to catch up with her. Helping Jessie didn't mean that they would have a repeat of their morning together. In the old days, when he came out to "help" her, he usually had rolling in the hay on his mind. The only thing on his mind today was…well, not rolling in the hay. Obviously not. But, damn, her walk was sexy.

JESSIE COULD FEEL Payson keeping pace beside her, really close beside her, so she kept her gaze forward. She refused to believe that she was happy to see him.

"Wait," Payson said, putting his hand on her forearm. "I need to ask you something."

Jessie didn't pull away. She looked at his hand and wondered why his touch felt different from anyone else's. She pulled herself together and said, "Go ahead."

He slowly stepped away, and Jessie noted the tense angle of his head. He opened his mouth, closed it and then took two long strides away from her. "When you were at my condo and we—"

"I'm not pregnant. That's what you wanted to ask, right?" She couldn't help her angry tone.

He whirled to her. For just a split second, his chestnut-brown eyes closed before he calmly answered, "You're certain? You took a test?"

"Didn't need a test."

"I see," he said. "It's for the best."

"Yes."

"A baby deserves two parents," Payson went on.

"Right, of course," Jessie said, crossing her arms over her chest.

"What?"

"Nothing."

"It's something. You have that look."

"I don't think you're right about a baby and two parents." She knew her feelings about not being pregnant were irrational and tangled up with the miscarriage and the end of their marriage.

"What do you mean?"

"I mean if I had been pregnant, I would have raised the baby myself, and she would have been happy."

"I wouldn't have let you do that," Payson said firmly.

"What do you mean you wouldn't have *let* me?" she asked, her tone soft but steely.

"If you had been pregnant, you would not have been alone. I would have been there, too, no matter what."

"You mean just like last time?"

"I was there last time. You were the one who pushed me away. We talked about this," he said, sounding frustrated and turning again from her. "It doesn't matter because you're not pregnant."

"You're right. It doesn't matter, but I am curious. You really think that you could be different this time?"

"We're older and wiser...I hope. We'd both treat a pregnancy very differently now."

Jessie nodded. If she'd been pregnant, she would have cherished every moment of morning sickness and every change in her body. "But I'm not pregnant," she finally said.

He stepped back to her, reached out and grasped her hand.

She hadn't realized that she needed the comfort of his touch. The warmth of his hand in hers made the stiffness of her posture relax.

Payson tugged on Jessie's hand, enfolding her in his arms. She didn't resist. She laid her head on his shoulder, her lips against his neck.

"I'm a little sad," he whispered.

"Me, too," she whispered. "I know it would have been a disaster, but I...I don't know what."

"We would have made it work because we know how precious a baby is." He pulled her more firmly against him, rocking a little.

Jessie didn't want to move. She didn't want the warmth of Payson's arms to disappear. She finally felt safe and whole again. Why was it that only his arms provided that? Why did his gentleness and strength make her feel this way? She couldn't answer that today. Her arms stayed clamped around him as she burrowed farther into his embrace.

"I need to get back to work," she said but didn't move.

"I'm supposed to help with that," he said, his voice rumbling through her chest.

Step back, get a grip and stand on your own two feet, her brain urged her. She started to pull back and Payson's arms tightened again.

"Not yet," he said into her hair. She relaxed again.

Payson couldn't name the mixture of regret, worry and panic that warmed the pit of his stomach. His lips brushed her hair as he took in her scent, trying to settle his mind. His body reacted swiftly as her hip grazed against him. Desire flashed through him, making his pulse pound. His mouth sought hers. The kiss deepened quickly, their tongues tangling, tasting, exploring. He pulled her more tightly into his grip. He wanted...more. He rocked his hips against hers.

Jessie's moan vibrated against his mouth and straight to his gut. His hand traveled up her body, cupping her breast, her perfect handful of a breast. His thumb brushed over the nipple pressed against all of the layers of cloth. Jessie nipped his lip and now he moaned. His other hand snaked up her back and held her head to his mouth, sealing their lips together.

Then he yanked at her cowgirl shirt, pulling it from her pants. He had to touch her silky skin. His hand skimmed along her waist and back to her breast. He nibbled at her jaw as the contact of her skin against his palm ignited him. His hand found its way inside her bra and the puckered nipple scraped against his surgeon-sensitive fingertips. His hips thrust forward against her.

Her hand pushed him back and he protested, then her clever fingers popped open the button on his jeans. He held his breath, then gasped at the first hiss of the zipper being lowered. *More. More now.* His chest heaved, trying to get the breath to tell her to not stop. A horse whinnied and another took up the call.

Just enough blood got to his brain for him to think clearly. What the heck were they doing? His hips froze. He dropped his hand, took a final deep breath of her scent and stepped away. *Get a grip on this, Payson.* He took another step and turned. Emotions roared through him and urged him to go back to her, take her right here. In the eerie quiet, he heard the sound of the snaps of her shirt. *Damn.* He banished the picture of what she covered with her cowgirl shirt.

The heat in his groin flared again. *Think, man.* He imagined the intricate surgery that he'd do tomorrow, the first incision and the delicate manipulation of the tendon and…finally, his hormones were safely corralled by his physician's control.

He cleared his throat and said in his professional, just-out-of-the-operating-room surgeon's voice—cool and unaffected, "Where do we start? Which horse?"

JESSIE REFUSED TO glare at Payson's all-powerful, I-never-lose-control doctor look. She could be just as collected. She forced a rodeo smile onto her face. No way she'd let him know that the kiss they'd just shared had weakened her knees and made her heart pound. She said without a tremor in her voice, "Each horse gets one flake of hay."

Not waiting for him to answer, she went to the feed bins to get the buckets ready. Far away from Payson. She just needed a few minutes for her heart to slow down.

That man can kiss. No one else made her want to curl up and be taken care of. No other man made her feel clingy and desperate for his approval, his notice. That was then, she told herself. Three years had made a big difference. She knew now she could do it all on her own—*and* that she could ask for help. Payson and his crew had helped with Hope's Ride and so had all of the volunteers, and she hadn't stopped being herself. Didn't she always tell the kids that they had to ask for help?

The kids. The ache deep inside her started again. She missed every one of them. Whatever did or did not happen with Payson only mattered when it affected Hope's Ride and all of those little children. So, feed the darned horses, lock everything up for the night and go back to Lavonda's to figure out how to get more money. No more thinking about Payson...or remembering what he could do to her in bed. Their relationship had to stay professional. She looked down at the bucket in her hand, no idea what she'd put in it. *Dang it.* Of course it was Molly's feed. Jessie glared at the contents. One bucket of mixed up food wouldn't kill the pony, especially considering the junk she normally ate.

Jessie concentrated on filling each bucket correctly. She didn't meet up with Payson until she put her last bucket in place. He stood in the aisle between the stalls, his dark, intense gaze on her. "What?" she asked, looking away because she didn't want to glimpse the heat that had been there earlier.

"Anything else you need done?" His voice remained cool, although she could see his shoulders were overly squared.

"That's it. I just have to lock up."

"I'll wait."

He didn't move and the need to fill the silence pressed down on her. "So…" She dragged out the word, groping for something to say. Something that had nothing to do with the scorching kiss they'd shared. "Lavonda's sure that the money will come pouring in, so I can get the bank off my back, which also means that I definitely won't need that money from the hospital. It won't be long until you and your crew are back here."

He nodded. She could feel his gaze on her. She fiddled with each stall-door lock as they walked out of the barn. She always double-checked them before she left and made sure that Molly and Bull's pen had the extra lock in place. "Since your job is safe and we'll be back at work soon with all of the donations we get, that promotion should be coming along, right?"

"That's the plan," he said.

"Good. The hospital will get a good director." She really meant that. She'd never doubted that he was good at his job. "Then you'll be too important to worry about Hope's Ride." That's what she prayed would happen. Her heart couldn't take the idea that he'd been helping her for any other reason.

"Since Desert Valley pediatric patients will use the facility, I'm sure I'll still be involved."

That was not what she wanted to hear, and she told her fluttering heart to stop being excited. "All done," she said with relief, moving as quickly as she could through the large sliding door. Of course, her quick exit went wrong when she stumbled on a bit of uneven ground. She couldn't stop the gasp. "It's nothing," she said quickly, catching her breath as the sharp pain dulled. Her knee actually had been better lately because her work days had gone from twelve hours to eight.

"I can get you an appointment."

"I know. Later. Once Hope's Ride is on its feet... No pun intended," she said, working hard not to limp. They stood at their vehicles—his barely dusty Range Rover and her beat-up pickup. "Thanks again for the help." Payson stood staring at her and she couldn't read his expression.

"Do you think if we'd gone and talked with someone we wouldn't have gotten divorced?" Payson asked, his voice level.

Her breath exploded out of her. This was not what she expected from him, and she had no idea how to answer him. "I don't...maybe." Sad as it made her to admit it. If they had worked a little harder, maybe they could have salvaged their marriage. Three years of distance allowed her to admit that now.

"That's what I think, too, especially..." He trailed off.

She didn't need him to say more. The kiss they'd just shared, yesterday's closeness and the morning at his condo—their sexual connection had stayed strong. "But we're divorced now, and we both have new lives. You're going to be director of pediatrics, and I'll run Hope's Ride. Our marriage is ancient history."

He didn't smile. He didn't move. For several moments,

their gazes were intent on each other, linking them and making her feel as if she'd come home. *Dear Lord. Not again.* She couldn't love him again. "See you, Payson. I'll call the hospital as soon as I know our reopening date." She hopped into the truck and made herself not look back.

Chapter Fourteen

"Since you haven't said anything about the call from Children's Hospital, I'm just going to ask," Helen said as she handed over another folder for him to sign. "Are you leaving?"

His pen hung poised over the stack of papers. "Why would you think I was leaving?"

"Because you got a call from the country's—maybe the world's—best children's hospital, and I can't imagine they were phoning to give a donation."

"Helen, there's nothing to say." He stared at the papers. He didn't want to talk about the call. He wanted to focus on his upcoming surgeries and his patients.

She carefully set down another pile of papers and pointed to where sticky notes told him to sign. "I cleared your schedule this afternoon so you can go out to Hope's Ride."

"Excuse me?"

"The grand reopening. Alex told me that you said that you'd be there to see him lead Molly in the horse parade. 'Like in a real rodeo' is what he said."

Of course, he knew that Hope's Ride had pulled through its crisis. Spence told him that the foreclosure had been cleared up. Payson had stayed away because he knew that seeing Jessie was just too dangerous. When they were together, he had trouble remembering they were divorced.

Plus, he'd been busy. Because Payson's team had been delayed for so long by the foreclosure, the hospital had moved on, focusing on other programs to investigate—programs not dogged by financial scandal or media-savvy cowgirls. The administration refused to read Payson's preliminary report recommending the endorsement. Hope's Ride would become just one of the many "alternative therapy programs that patients are welcome to investigate but are not, at this time, seen as medically necessary."

On top of that, with Hope's Ride out, Payson's own promotion had evaporated. He'd been the one overseeing the program, then that same program had put the hospital in an ugly and untenable light.

Spence had let him know Jessie had enough to pay off the mortgage and then some, but Payson worried about what would happen in the long term.

"You cleared my schedule?" he asked, when what Helen had said cut through his brain fog.

"Yes."

"I don't remember me asking you to do that."

"Of course you didn't. Right now, you'd forget to eat if I didn't remind you. I knew you wouldn't want to disappoint Alex," she said, snatching up the stacks of papers and giving him a motherly I-know-best smile.

"That's a low blow, using Alex," he said.

She shrugged. "You need to get out of the office. I know you've slept here at least two nights. Settle what is going on between you and that ex-wife of yours."

She walked out of the office before he could say anything else.

Damn it. He stood to follow Helen. But for what? To ream her out? Yeah, that would work. Then she'd quit and where would he be? Drowning in even more paperwork. He turned back to the desk and sat down to finish up his case notes because apparently he was going to Hope's Ride this afternoon…for Alex. From the beginning, his connection with the little boy had been different. Payson hadn't been able to keep the usual distance he put between himself and his patients, which in the course of treatments allowed him to make split-second decisions in the operating room. One afternoon watching him at the program would be fine. He could say hello to Jessie—just hello—and wish her luck.

They wouldn't be alone, and it was past time to move on, as he'd often heard these past three years. Anything else he'd felt since working with Jessie had been strictly a physical reaction based on proximity and memory. When he no longer saw Jessie, he'd totally forget about the feel of her skin and his instant flash of desire when they touched.

PAYSON WATCHED ALEX and the other children march past, leading the horses, ponies and dogs in a short parade. As soon as he congratulated Alex and the other children he knew, Payson would head back to the hospital. He waved to the excited Alex, who stood behind Jessie as she announced the reopening of the ranch and thanked everyone. Payson got up. He had to get out of there. Seeing Jessie with the kids restarted the painful ache in his chest. He'd catch up with Alex as he came out of the building to take the pony back to her stall.

The desert heat pounded down on him. He looked for a bit of shade somewhere and wandered over to the barn. The overhang created a bar of cooler space, and he could easily see the arena. Watching Alex and the other children reminded him of why he'd chosen pediatric surgery. The difference he could and did make in their lives always humbled him. It also broke his heart when he couldn't help. He never let it show, but the detachment he kept in place during each surgery and consult crumbled anytime he had to say there was nothing more he could do. Today, though, he'd concentrate on the successes. Would those successes be sweeter in Philadelphia?

The hospital there had made him a great offer, including not only a directorship but also his own budget for research. The downsides were that it was thousands of miles from the patients he had now, and he wouldn't directly treat the children. On the other hand, at such a big hospital he would have the chance to make a difference in more children's lives.

He'd always planned that his work and sacrifices would lead to an executive position at a big research-and-teaching hospital where he would have control over an entire program. So that goal was right there. He just had to pick up the phone, say yes and he'd have his dream job. It'd mean that he and Jessie would never see each other again. The final link to her and their shared past would be severed. That's what he wanted, too, he told himself for the hundredth time. He'd make the call as soon as he got back to his office.

Faint applause brought his focus back to the corral. The parade was over. Time to see Alex and Jessie, too. After all, this would be the last chance to speak with her, because once she found out about Desert Valley's decision, she wouldn't spit on him if he were on fire.

JESSIE LOOKED OVER the children, parents, staff and volunteers as they clapped at the end of her very, very short speech. She gave a real smile, not one of her bright, false, rodeo ones. She could hardly believe that just weeks ago she'd lived through the second-worst day of her life—kicked off her property, locked out of her house and faced with bankruptcy. According to Lavonda, this grand reopening was just the start of what Jessie needed to do to keep the program solvent, even with the hospital's support. And she was still mostly sure about that support—in spite of the rumors she'd heard. She had to talk to Payson about that when the parade was over.

Lavonda's advice had been to not put all of her eggs in one basket, suggesting Jessie seek similar affiliations with other hospitals, too. Jessie tried not to be overwhelmed by her sister's enthusiasm. Jessie didn't remember Lavonda being quite this intense when they were growing up. She really didn't know how the other woman did it. Raising money tired Jessie out more than a full day of cleaning out stalls. Lavonda was always chipper after hours on the phone asking for money.

Jessie signaled for the lead volunteer to have the children parade out of the arena. The standing ovation made Jessie a little misty. She pulled herself together and followed the parade to make sure the animals got back to the proper stalls and the overexcited children didn't get into any trouble.

"Miss Jessie, Miss Jessie," Alex yelled to her, waving his arm.

She hurried to the boy. He grinned widely, holding

tight to Molly's lead rope. The little pony had been decorated with ribbons in her mane and flowers entwined in her halter. She'd become a minor celebrity, her picture featured prominently on the ranch's new website. Molly had taken to being a star like the diva she was.

Jessie squatted down gingerly, her knee creaking, and gave Alex a hug. He squeezed her hard. She inhaled deeply, taking in his little-boy scent of candy and dust. For a moment her heart clenched, and then she let him go.

"We decorated Molly good, didn't we?" he asked.

"You sure did," Jessie said, patting the pony on the head and admiring the bows that Alex had tied "all by myself." She listened as Alex explained what he'd done while Hope's Ride was not open. Jessie hadn't noticed that they were not alone until she heard Alex cry, "Dr. Mac!"

"Alex." Payson's deep voice was gentle.

"Look what I did, Dr. Mac," Alex said, grabbing Payson's hand and turning him to Molly. The little guy repeated what he had told Jessie about his work on prettying up the pony.

"You did a very good job," Payson said. "Did you pretty up Miss Jessie, too?"

"Silly. Miss Jessie is always pretty."

"You may be right," Payson said.

She turned again to Alex, afraid to meet her ex-husband's eyes after the last time they'd been together. "Thank you, Alex," she said, concentrating on not noticing how close Payson was. "That is very nice of you to say."

"Here," Alex said, handing Molly's lead rope to her. "Connor is here." She watched as he walked nearly as fast as a normal little boy toward his friend, who was in a motorized wheelchair.

"I've got to take care of Molly," Jessie said and started to move away from Payson.

"Wait," he said, laying a hand on her arm.

The pony stomped her dainty hoof, just missing Payson's loafer-clad foot. With a glare at his shoes, she moved the pony to her other side. "I need to get Miss Thing here to her adoring public."

"What?"

"Molly has gotten used to being the center of attention. When all of this hoopla dies down, I don't know what we're going to do with her."

Payson didn't respond and didn't move, standing much too close, making it hard to concentrate on what she wanted to say. "I've got to get her to the pen where everyone can fuss over her. I'm glad I saw you because I do need to speak with you. As soon as Molly is settled, we can talk."

He started to open his mouth and she said, "I'll share Mama's *dulce de leche* brownies." The gooey, caramely treats were Payson's favorites, and her mother only made them for very special occasions, like the grand reopening and when they'd announced Jessie's pregnancy.

"Lead on," he said, but he didn't look happy.

She tugged Molly forward and made the pony hurry as much as the stubborn little animal would allow. Jessie could feel Payson behind her, not his usual detached, calm self. Taking him back to the house would be a bad idea, she decided. "We can just talk here."

"Are you trying to get out of sharing the brownies?" he asked, a half smile on his face.

"Maybe," she said, relaxing into a grin. "Fine, give me a minute." She hurried Molly into the pen, where she could be admired by her fans.

Jessie and Payson entered the ranch house through the kitchen, which was a mess of dirty dishes and papers. In the rush to get ready for the grand reopening, Jessie's less-than-stellar housekeeping skills had disappeared as she focused on all of the other details. The brownies were hidden in the microwave. She pulled them out and looked through cupboards for a container to give him a couple of pieces to take along.

"I'll just eat them here," he said holding out a hand.

"You can bring them home. This won't take long."

"Hand 'em over."

His greed startled a laugh out of Jessie. "Would you like milk or something?" she asked as he cut a large brownie from the pan and took a huge bite. He shook his head and then closed his eyes in obvious bliss. "Maybe I should leave you alone with them?"

He swallowed and said, "These are so wrong, they're right. How can ancho chilies make them taste so good?"

Jessie shrugged and watched as Payson took another bite and chewed with delight. His legs were braced and his shoulders relaxed. This was the man she remembered. The one she'd married, ignoring their parents' advice to wait until Payson finished med school. This was the man who was confident, not arrogant. He was the man who loved the fact that Jessie could do things on her own, that she didn't rely on him for every single thing in her life. When had he changed? Or had it been her?

"All right," Payson said, eying the pan of goodies but not cutting another piece. "Before you tell me what you need to tell me, I wanted to let you know that you've done an amazing job here. Raising the money, getting everything settled with the bank. Good for you."

He actually did sound proud. "Thanks, it's been tough, but I just kept thinking about the kids."

"I know what you mean. Every time I get called in the middle of the night or feel too exhausted to talk to one more family, that's what I think about."

She nodded. Her throat clogged with emotion. Of course he understood. Even if he had bigger plans for his career, he'd always been devoted to the children under his care. That was one of the reasons it had been so devastating when they'd lost their baby. *That was yesterday*, she told herself. Sad as it was, they both had lives and new children to nurture. She looked at him and her heart filled with a warmth that made her want to grin like an idiot.

"Speaking of children," he said, his face firming into the "doctor" look that she knew so well. He pulled out his phone and glanced at the screen. "I've got to go. Call me later."

She watched him hurry across the yard in his very uncowboy loafers and thought he looked more powerful and competent than any other man she knew, even her daddy. She looked away, noticing he hadn't taken any more brownies with him. Darn it. She'd wrap up the goodies and take them to the hospital. She didn't want the treats here or she'd eat the whole pan. Plus, she hadn't gotten to ask him about the rumors. Payson might have done a ton of things during their marriage that made her crazy, but he never lied. If she asked him about the hospital, he'd tell her the truth.

Chapter Fifteen

Of course, no one was ready to leave the fun at Hope's Ride, which meant that by the time Jessie could get away, Payson had left. She debated going to his house. She'd promised him brownies, plus she *had* to get her questions answered.

She pulled into his driveway and sat for a moment, calming the flutter in her stomach. Too much cake at the party. She walked to the front door and caught the bright gleam of light through the shutters. He was definitely home. Good. She pushed the doorbell. What if he was on the patio? Would he hear the bell? She shifted and felt the twinge in her knee. The aspirin had dulled the sharpness, but maybe Payson was right and—

"Jessie?" Payson asked, opening the door in only well-worn jeans.

Dang it. The familiar tight flutter low in her abdomen started up and made her catch her breath as she took in every inch of him. "I…you forgot your brownies," she said lamely, thrusting the plastic container at him, hitting his bare stomach.

His hands automatically closed around the container and her hand. "Thanks," he said in a gruff voice.

Her gaze locked onto his, and she saw the once-familiar flash of heat. She savored the graceful power of his fingers on hers and the clean, just-out-of-the-shower scent of him. She wanted him. Reluctantly, she pulled her hand from his. They stood inches apart. *Step away.* She had to stop her libido right now. She licked her lips. Her mouth dried as she heard Payson cut off a groan.

"Do you want to come in?" he asked, his knuckles whitening as his hand clenched around the plastic container. His expression didn't show any emotion, happy or mad.

The polite distance of his invitation broke the spell. She nodded and stepped past him. In the narrowness of the doorway, she imagined he leaned toward her and thought for sure he'd kiss her, but he didn't.

"I called the hospital," she said in a matching cool, impersonal tone. "They said you'd left." She walked into his living room, unsure of her next step. Why had she agreed to stay? The rumors. She had to ask about the rumors.

"Sit down. I can get you a drink, and we'll share the brownies."

"No," she said, more sharply than she'd meant to. She didn't want to sit on *the* couch. She glanced up at him and saw the memory of that morning reflected in his eyes. "I can't stay long," she added more calmly. "I just needed to ask you something, then I'll go."

He nodded and shifted the plastic container to his other hand.

Distracted by his lack of shirt and the well-defined muscles of his lightly haired chest, she glanced away. "I heard a rumor from a parent, who heard it from one of the therapists at the hospital, who'd apparently heard from an administrative assistant—"

"I know how the rumor mill works."

"I just wanted you to know that I understand it's just a rumor, but I have to ask…is the hospital going to end the arrangement with Hope's Ride, even though I took care of the foreclosure?" He didn't need to say anything. She saw the answer in his eyes. "Why didn't you say anything?"

"Because we were ordered to keep it confidential. Leaked information wouldn't have just affected me. Other people's jobs were on the line."

"Confidential from me? I'm the one they're going to screw."

"You're set financially now."

"But the hospital's endorsement is important, essential for the program to keep operating long term."

"I still shouldn't be confirming anything. I told you how the hospital is about employees. Plus, not knowing let you celebrate your achievement. Raising enough to keep Hope's Ride running isn't a small thing."

Her jaw ached from clenching her teeth. Payson didn't get it. She had a right to know. He had said other jobs were on the line, though. Could she fault him for protecting his coworkers? "Okay." She laughed when she saw the surprise in his eyes. "I'm totally freaked out, but you're right. I did get through the foreclosure. With help, I saved Hope's Ride. So I think I can get through anything the hospital throws at me."

"I need to sit down."

"Ha-ha." They stood for a moment more, taking in the shifting dynamic and the blessed relaxation of the tension. "I want to hear what you can tell me. What you think *might* happen. Forewarned is forearmed."

"Go ahead and take a seat. I need an iced tea. You sure you don't want one?"

"That would be nice."

"What about dinner?" he asked as he walked toward the kitchen. "I haven't eaten. I know you had food at the party, but you probably only ate the cake. You need real food."

"I'm good." She'd never admit that he was right about the cake. If she did that, who knew what Payson would do? The shock of her saying he was right twice in one night might put him into cardiac arrest.

She heard him down the hall, and she kept her gaze glued to his bookshelves. She noted the photos of Payson with his patients, as well as the two formal portraits of his family in their living room. The MacCormack house screamed designer Old West.

"Here," Payson said, handing her a glass and motioning for her to take a seat.

She turned and saw that he'd been busy in the kitchen. Paper plates of nachos, chicarrones—his favorite wheel-shaped, fried pork rinds—and cheese, along with containers of guacamole, salsa and jars of olives and pickles covered the coffee table. She noted that he hadn't included the brownies and, more importantly, he'd put on a shirt.

"I hope you're hungry," she said to cover her increasing nervousness.

"A little bit," he said and pulled a pile of nachos onto a paper towel that served as his napkin and dinner plate. He added a big spoonful of guacamole and shoved the mess into his mouth.

She couldn't tear her eyes away from Payson. What could be sexy about eating nachos? Nothing. Her brother

and men all over Phoenix ate the same snack. *Move
along. Nothing sexy here.* Hoping to get her mind back on
the important stuff—the only stuff that should matter—
she asked, "Why does the hospital want to break off its
work with me? I did what you asked in the interview."

"Time, tide and Desert Valley waits for no man…
woman. The delay because of the foreclosure threat took
too long to resolve. They moved on to other projects, but
they will say that Hope's Ride is an alternative that patients are welcome to seek out."

"So it's not the program?"

He shook his head and created another pile of nachos.

"That's nice to know, but unless the doctors and the
parents *and* the insurance companies know that we're
legitimate, I could be back to the same place in another
year. I still need the endorsement from the hospital."

He stopped eating. "There are other hospitals in Phoenix."

"That'll take too long," she barked. "There are also
a number of donors lending their support because we're
an 'approved' program."

"What does that even mean?"

"Lavonda suggested it. We had the hospital employees
at the ranch. You were there. It certainly looked like the
Desert Valley had given us the thumbs-up."

Jessie could see the thoughts flitting across Payson's
familiar face. He shook his head and said, "The decision
has been made. They're just determining the best way
to announce it. You probably have a little bit of time."

Jessie leaned back on the couch, suddenly tired at the
idea of going to another hospital and convincing more
doctors and therapists of the value of Hope's Ride. She'd
been so sure her big troubles were behind her, but, of

course, nothing could be that simple. The task felt too big to think about tonight.

"Don't fall asleep," Payson said anxiously.

Her eyes popped open. "I wasn't sleeping. I was thinking."

"Have something to eat. You'll feel better." He pushed a plate of cheese toward her.

Her stomach gurgled. Cake might not have been the best choice for her main meal. She popped a piece of cheese into her mouth and chased it with a couple of chile-stuffed olives. They ate companionably, and she was thankful that he didn't want to talk. When she drank the last of her iced tea, she actually felt energized. "Thanks," she said as she stood to throw away her paper-towel plate.

"Don't worry about cleaning up."

She laughed. "It's the least I can do since you fed me."

She walked the ten steps to the kitchen and felt Payson right behind her. She should be worried about Hope's Ride, the hospital and her future. All of those worries were there somewhere at the back of her mind, but as they'd eaten, the memory of Payson's touch filled her mind. His competent and clever surgeon hands on her waist, her stomach, her breasts—right there on that couch.

She found the garbage can under the sink, just as it had been in every place they'd lived. When she turned, he was close, reaching around her to throw something into the can. They were face-to-face, her back against the counter. She couldn't move…didn't want to move.

This is what you want, that traitorous part of her whispered. She couldn't hide from the truth. She wanted Payson. Her program could be going to crap and she still wanted him. Just like always, when Payson was around, she saw nothing but him.

She wrapped her arms around him, pulling him against her so they fit together as they always had. His hips nestled into hers, heating her and at the same time feeling like home. This was exactly where she should be.

"Jessie," he whispered into her hair. His hand moved from her waist up her body to cup her breast. "So lovely."

Her laugh turned into a gasp as his hand squeezed her sensitized breast. The nipple rubbed almost painfully against the fabric of her bra. Her leg moved behind him, and she barely felt the twinge in her knee as she pulled him closer with her strong thigh. She held him against her, even as he shifted. She didn't want him to move away. She didn't want to have a chance to change her mind.

She found his mouth with hers, exploring every inch. The touch and the taste of him arrowed down, making her lift her hips against him. His hands moved lower, cupping her butt. She yanked his shirt up, desperate to get her hands on his skin, his sleekly moving muscles. She shivered with delight when the air brushed against her own skin. Magically, her bra was gone; his shirt was gone. She brushed her nipples against the hair that furred his chest, quivering with delight.

"Can't wait," he hissed as his clever fingers opened the snap of her jeans, slipped inside and brushed over her.

"Payson. No teasing," she said with feeling, pushing against his fingers.

He chuckled, deep and sexy. "You love my teasing." He nipped at her neck and cheek as his fingers went deeper. She couldn't stop the moan. Her hips pushed against him, and he rubbed his thumb against her aching nub. The heat built and she wanted more. Her fingers now frantically worked at his pants, joined by his as he grabbed at his back pocket. "A man can hope—" he said, holding out the condom.

She didn't hesitate in stepping out of her own jeans as Payson pushed them down, knelt and kissed her right where her ache was centered. Then he stood, lifting her easily onto the counter, as he put on protection. He plunged in. She wrapped her legs around him, making sure that he stayed tight against her even as he rocked and bucked them to completion. She arched her back and cried out as he shuddered.

Payson's breathing slowed. Jessie felt the cold hardness of the countertop. She wiggled. Payson kissed her tenderly. "That was an appetizer," he said, pulling away reluctantly from the kiss. When he finally lifted her from the counter, she tightened her legs around him again so she didn't fall as he carried her down the hall.

"I have to have you again, but I want to take my time," Payson said as he laid her down on his bed and turned on the bedside light. Jessie opened her mouth to tell him to turn it off, then the light fell across Payson, highlighting the strength of his body and the excitement he felt. She wanted to see every inch of him. She wanted to remember this night.

"You're in charge," she whispered, arching her back to offer herself to him.

"Really?" he said, kneeling on the bed, stroking her breast. "You're giving yourself to me? You're admitting that *you* need *me*?"

"I need you…now," she said pulling him to her.

"Good."

She gasped in delight as his breath puffed over her skin. Her brain scrambled to come up with words. Instead she used her hands and her mouth to tell him what she needed. But Payson anticipated her every move until the two of them were joined again. They rocked together, the heat building and building until Jessie shattered, only coming to herself when she heard Payson whisper, "Jessie, my love, my cowgirl." Then his weight held her to the mattress. Her arms went tight around him, and she nuzzled his neck, her lips brushing along his roughened jaw as she drifted into sleep, contented and happy.

PAYSON SLID FROM the bed as light filtered through the plantation-style shutters. He didn't want to get up. He wanted to snuggle against Jessie and take her again. He kept moving, for once not pushing away the memories of their marriage—how he'd refused to let anything come between him and his patients, including his wife. Jessie'd said she understood that passion because she had the same commitment to the rodeo. But how could he think that leaving before she crawled out of bed and coming home long after she was asleep was a good way to keep a marriage alive? On top of that, he'd missed three of her birthdays in a row and nearly every one of their anniversaries.

He stepped into the shower, wondering what he would do differently if he and Jessie were married now. First, he would wake her with kisses instead of stealing out of bed. Second, he would make time for the two of them and he wouldn't spend that precious time arguing about the amount of money she spent on horse feed.

So, hotshot doc, what are you going to do about today?

Had he and Jessie started something? Or was this just the two of them reliving their past…again? He let the water pound on him, hoping it would help him come up with an answer. The connection with Jessie hadn't changed. In fact, it had gotten stronger. So what the heck was he going to do about that?

Get out of the shower and talk with her.

He could live with that as a plan. He hurried out of the shower, toweled off and went to the bedroom. Jessie wasn't there. He pulled on clothing and rushed into the living room. He relaxed as soon as he saw her standing in front of the coffeemaker, watching it intently. He smiled. Jessie never spoke or moved faster than a cud-chewing cow until she'd downed her first cup of coffee.

"Hey," he said softly. "You know a watched coffee pot never drips."

She grunted an answer. He slipped in behind her, wrapping his arms around her. She didn't pull away but leaned into him. His groin tightened as her butt pushed against him. He looked at the clock on the stove. They might have enough time. He nibbled at her neck and cupped her breast through his T-shirt. God. She looked sexy in the thin shirt emblazoned with the Desert Valley Hospital logo. She hummed and he pulled her tighter. Suddenly, she turned in his arms and her mouth latched on to his, tasting him, her body molding to him so that he forgot everything but her.

"Almost as good as coffee," she said with a saucy grin as she pulled away.

"Wow. I feel honored. I'm on the same level with coffee."

"Almost." She poured herself a cup and one for him, too, then sidled past. His gaze was glued to the hem of

the shirt, hoping to see just a glimpse of her lovely nakedness. She sat at the bar, took two long swallows of
coffee and stared at him. "So…"

He sipped his coffee, letting her start this conversation. He knew she complained that he always wanted to
be in control. Not today. He would let her take the lead.

"What was last night?" she asked when he remained
silent.

"Terrific? Spectacular?"

He didn't like the rodeo smile she gave him as she
said, "That's not what I mean. One time sleeping together is bad judgment." She took a slug of coffee. "Two
times is either stupidity, craziness or…"

"What do you want it to be?"

"I don't know, especially with everything else that's
going on."

"I don't want to be accused of taking control but can
I say what I don't want this to be?" he asked.

She nodded and buried her face in the cup.

"I don't want it to be a one-night stand or a hookup.
Okay?" She nodded again. "I don't want to tell anyone
about it yet…not because I'm ashamed or anything, but
because I want this to be ours. I don't want to have to
justify or explain."

He put up his hand to stop her as she opened her
mouth to speak, his gaze locked onto hers. "I have no
idea where this may lead, but for once, I'm fine with
just taking the ride. I want you in my bed again, and
I would take you there right now but I've got to get to
work. And I'm not saying that to get away. I have surgery and rounds. I expect to see you tonight. I'll be sure
to get up early enough to give you a better good morning tomorrow."

He moved around the bar and kissed her forehead. God. He didn't want to leave her now or…ever. What a mess. Philly had moved front and center in his future and now Jessie—

"Actually, I just wanted to ask you to pour me more coffee," she said with another one of those saucy grins that tightened his groin. Why did he love it so much when she was being a big pain in his butt? "But, Payson, this is probably the worst time for me to get involved with you or anyone."

"You're not getting involved with anyone else."

She patted his hand and stood up. "Everything is so up in the air. I know what Mama would tell me. 'Baby girl, when your plate is full, you eat that first before you go back for dessert.'"

"That doesn't even make sense."

"You're my dessert. I shouldn't be having you before I deal with my very full plate, but I just can't resist," she said quietly, hugging him to her and kissing him.

Her soft lips and gifted tongue were sugary sweet from her coffee and a taste that was all Jessie. His hand slid under the hem of the shirt she wore, cupping her bare bottom. "You really are testing my self-control, aren't you?" he asked in a hoarse whisper.

"Hmm…I was just sittin' here havin' my mornin' coffee when some man came up and started kissin' on me." She brushed her thumbs over his cheekbones, her sage-green gaze searching his face. "This is the best morning I've had in three years."

"Me, too." He kissed her hard this time, wanting to put some kind of mark on her so that all day she'd remember this, him, them.

Chapter Sixteen

Jessie sang along at the top of her lungs when Blake Shelton came on her Scout's battered radio. Her cheeks actually hurt from smiling. She'd need to settle down and get herself under control before facing the kids and the volunteers. An hour alone cleaning out stalls should take care of any lingering Payson effect.

She pulled into the ranch happier than she'd been in years—since before she and Payson divorced. Remembering that sobered her a little bit.

Don't borrow trouble, she told herself, because she already had plenty of that. Her conversation with Payson about the hospital reminded her that Hope's Ride wasn't as safe as she'd imagined, even with the bank off her back. She made a mental note to ask her sister to help—which would stun Lavonda—with more fundraisers. She'd also ask Payson if he could suggest another hospital to approach for support. He'd know the other medical types who'd be open to the program. Her stomach did a little dip when she thought about him. She'd made the first move last night, dropping off the brownies, even though until the moment she kissed him, she would have denied that. The real problem was that she didn't know what any of this meant. They were divorced. Wasn't that the end of things?

Her phone vibrated in her pocket. So much for having time to herself. "Hello, this is Jessie," she said into the phone, not recognizing the number.

"Ms. Leigh, I'm calling for Dr. Naill from Desert Valley."

Now her stomach dropped as dread filled her. When Payson had talked about the administration deciding against the endorsement, she'd thought she'd have more time before the hospital made the decision final. "How may I help you?"

"I'm to set up a meeting to discuss Hope's Ride. Dr. Naill and the administrative staff have time available on Friday or Wednesday of next week."

Get it over with or give herself time to come up with a plan…time to talk with Payson and ask for help from Lavonda and Spence? "Next Wednesday would work." They finalized the details and the location.

As soon as she ended the call, Jessie went with her first instinct and called Payson. She needed to hear his voice for reassurance that everything would work out, no matter how crappy it felt right now. The call went to voice mail, and she guessed he was in surgery or doing rounds. She left a message and then turned back to cleaning the stalls, hoping that by the time the volunteers and staff arrived she'd have calmed down, ready to tackle the day and Desert Valley.

LATE THAT AFTERNOON, Jessie, Payson, Lavonda and Spence sat at Jessie's dining table—a picnic table she'd painted a rich burnt orange to match the little cowboy hats on the curtains her mother had made. She rubbed her hand over the glossy surface, thinking about what Spence had just said.

"So the hospital can drop me like a hot potato and I don't have a choice?"

"That's about it," he said. "Which is why you should have had an attorney who would have required a written contract. As it is, they're under no obligation to follow through on any promises made by my brother or anyone else from the hospital."

"That advice isn't very helpful right now," she snapped back. Under the table, Payson squeezed her hand. She relaxed slightly.

"Cut her a break," Lavonda defended Jessie. "She thought a hospital was a place that wanted to *help* people. Silly her."

Payson put up his hand to stop Lavonda from going on. "There's got to be something you can do. It's breach of good faith or something?"

"Stick with doctorin'," Spence said in his fake drawl. "I'll look through everything you've given me. We might be able to push them with the threat of a defamation suit. Their sudden withdrawal could be interpreted as a commentary on the program and that could mean—"

Jessie brightened. "So you might be able to make them follow through."

"I'm not that good," Spence said. "The best we can probably hope for is an agreement to make a positive referral to any other hospital or provider if contacted about Hope's Ride, but you might also be required to sign a gag order in exchange for that."

"What?" Lavonda asked, leaning forward a little to get in Spence's face. "More with the hospital stopping Jessie from exercising her First Amendment rights."

Payson broke in, "Let's get back to Wednesday's meeting. We're all agreed that it's about Desert Valley rejecting the endorsement of Hope's Ride, which means that Jessie needs to find a new hospital. I had Helen do a little research. I just didn't have—"

Jessie pulled her hand away from Payson. "Helen?"

"She's discreet and she knows your program."

Jessie took a deep breath. She had to let them help her. She couldn't do this alone. "What did she find?"

"Arizona General is interested, and they're willing to send a sample agreement, which Spence can look over. If you sign a contract with the hospital, then you'll avoid getting yourself into another mess like this one. I talked with them, too. Logistically, it might be—"

"Excuse me," Jessie said carefully at the same time Lavonda said, "Oh, crap."

"I didn't agree to anything specific," Payson said. "You and Spence can go over the paperwork."

"Just because you didn't sign on the dotted line for me, you think it's okay?" Jessie asked carefully to keep her voice from rising.

"Jeez, Payson, I thought you were a genius," Spence said.

"What did I do now?" Payson asked, looking truly bewildered.

Jessie reined in her temper and took three seconds to think. She focused on Payson, ignoring everyone else in the room. "I know I'm *slightly* unreasonable about Hope's Ride," she said, working on a smile. "I can accept that you want to help and make sure that everything works out. And you are a genius, but this is the place that your IQ falls way below even marginally smart. I know

I need to be more gracious about accepting help, but maybe you need to be willing to give up a little control."

"I wasn't trying to control you, Jessie. I really just wanted to help."

"I know that," she said and picked up his hand again. The tightness in her chest loosened as the anger drained out of her. "Next time, talk with me first."

"Next time?"

"There will be a next time and another next time. And you'll remember that sometimes I'm a little too independent and you'll cut me a break, all right?"

He snorted a little laugh and squeezed her hand. "I've always admired your cowgirl independence. It's just sometimes…"

"I know I need to ask for help, not just so I don't hurt myself or someone else, but because people really do want to help. It can be a gift to them as much as to me." She sucked in breath. "You awed me with the way you took control in the toughest situations, but that wasn't always what I needed or what anyone else needs. I know you're just trying to protect us from any harm, but we all need to stumble to get it right. The kids at Hope's Ride fall and they do things wrong all of the time. That's when they learn the most and feel the proudest. Just let me be wrong sometimes. And then don't say I told you so."

He laughed out loud this time. "I might be able to do that."

"Great," interrupted Spence, his tone sharp. "You've had your Dr. Phil moment. Can we get on with saving this damned program?"

"Who crapped in your corn flakes?" Lavonda shot back.

"Darlin'," Spence started, his cowboy drawl more pronounced. "I've got a job and a life—"

Jessie said quickly, "While we wait to see what Desert Valley does and what Arizona General offers, Lavonda will work on more fund-raising ideas. Spence will go through all of the agreements with a fine-toothed comb and Payson will perform surgical miracles." She smiled at him. "And I'll keep Hope's Ride running."

"Guess we all know who's in charge now," Payson said.

"You betcha." Jessie hoped she sounded a lot more confident than she felt.

When Lavonda and Spence walked out, it seemed natural for Jessie and Payson to stand on the porch and say good-night. It felt even better when he stayed the night with her. The week of waiting for the appointment would be a lot easier with Payson around.

JESSIE SAT IN Dr. Naill's office, the hospital's president, with Spence, wishing she was with Payson instead. She'd actually let Spence do most of the talking, only chiming in when he gave her a nod. It was killing her to not tell these suits to go shove it. But Lavonda had pointed out that while Arizona was a big state, the medical community was small. She couldn't afford to burn any of her bridges.

The attorney for the board said, "We would reconsider our position, but as Dr. MacCormack is moving his practice to Philadelphia Children's Hospital, we don't have the internal expertise…"

The words became a buzzing sound in her brain. Jessie could only focus on the fact that without saying one word to her, Payson had decided to leave. Everything he'd said and done in the past week had made her think that they were moving toward…reconciliation.

"Thank you," Spence said, and Jessie felt a tug on her arm.

"Yes, thank you," she replied automatically. This was why she should rely only on herself. Of course he would do what was best for his career. He always had. Her job had been second, her needs had been third or fourth. She'd go to the ranch and take a ride, work the horses, hang out with the kids. All of that would get her through the next few hours. Then she'd go to Payson's condo and tell him to take a hike. She didn't need any more of his help or his connections. He probably had sabotaged the offer from Arizona General, just as he had Desert Valley's.

"What the hell are you thinking?" Spence asked as he hustled her down a hall.

"Molly needs new shoes."

"You're lying. You're thinking of ways to get back at Payson."

She shook her head, beyond anger and hurt. "Really. I've got this long list of chores for the ranch."

"He didn't say anything to me either. Those guys were probably bluffing to remove any liability. I won't—"

"I don't think so," she said dully.

"Give my big-brained but stupid brother a chance to explain. I know I wasn't always your fan, but seeing you two together again…" He trailed off.

"It's so like him. To make a decision and tell me about it later." She refused to spend more of her energy and emotions on Payson.

"Payson would not leave you high and dry. Look at everything's he done to make sure you succeeded. He came clean about all of it. Why would he take a job in Philadelphia and not tell any of us?"

She stayed silent. Spence could be right. She finally took a deep breath to settle her speeding heart. He deserved the benefit of her doubt. He'd definitely earned that.

JESSIE STOOD AT the threshold of the barn, listening to Payson speak with a little girl as she got up the courage to pat Molly.

"Now, Doris, I'm going to take your hand and put it on Molly's mane." The little girl squeaked. Jessie stepped forward but stopped when she saw Payson gently drop the girl's hand. "I won't make you touch her. But I know Molly would like to be petted, wouldn't you, Molly?" The pony obligingly nodded her head, making her mane fly. Doris shrank back. As always, Jessie could read Payson's thoughts on his face. Not one iota of irritation showed.

"Watch, I'll pet her first." He put his large, nimble surgeon's fingers on the pony. He gave her three or four strokes. "Do you want to try? How about if you put your hand right on top of mine?" Doris inched closer to Payson, her inky-black hair pulled into a ponytail that had started to straggle down her back. Her round cheeks glistened with tear tracks. He didn't move as she crept closer and reached out. Molly stood stock-still.

"Did you touch her?" Payson whispered. Jessie saw the girl's hand brush against the mane. Her eyes widened in surprise.

"Soft."

"Miss Jessie uses special shampoo to make it pretty and soft. Just like your mommy does with your hair."

Doris stepped away from Payson and now Jessie could see the prosthetic fitted to her lower leg. The little girl had been with the program less than a week and today was the first time Jessie had seen her with the new leg. After petting Molly's mane, she gave the pony a hug. Molly nibbled her hair. Payson remained crouched, ready to spring forward to protect the little girl. Instead, she giggled and even let the pony sniff her metal leg.

Jessie turned away. She didn't want either of them to see the tears in her eyes. How could she ever have imagined that he'd abandon them? The hospital bigwigs were wrong. Payson would never leave his patients. Now, she hoped that he'd never leave her, either.

PAYSON SEARCHED THE BARN and arena for Jessie. He'd seen her earlier when he and Doris petted Molly, then she'd disappeared. He wanted to know how the meeting had gone. When he couldn't find her right away, he'd tried Spence but had gotten his voice mail. Anxiety knotted his gut. The only reason he could imagine that he couldn't find Jessie or reach Spence was that the meeting had gone worse than they'd all prepared for. If he didn't find her in the house, he'd start his search over.

He walked into the kitchen and Jessie raced across the room and into his arms. She kissed him hard and clutched at his shoulders. "I'm sorry. So sorry." Her voice was tear soaked.

"Oh, my God, Jessie. What's happened? Is it Alex?"

"No," she said shaking her head violently. "I'm so sorry that I doubted you. I've treated you so badly when all you ever wanted to do was help."

Payson froze, unsure how to react. Jessie didn't cry. Jessie didn't apologize. He patted her back and murmured something as he tried to figure out what to say to her. The meeting must have been a total bust. When she quieted, he said, "I know you had been counting on Desert Valley, but we made plans for the hospital dropping the program. You've got Spence and Lavonda and all of the other volunteers to keep things going. Plus, we've got a chance with Arizona General."

"It's not Hope's Ride. It's you. I always expect the worst of you, always expect you to act the way you did when we were young, but we've changed, both of us. I understand," she said, taking his face in her hands, her warm green gaze holding his, her mouth curving. "I saw you today with Doris, and I knew that you weren't leaving us. Everything you've done is because you care so much about me and the kids."

His couldn't catch his breath. Her mouth reached for his, her lips softly loving his. His arms wrapped around her, heat building between them. The glow in his heart had him fighting tears. "Jessie, my sweet cowgirl, my stubborn, independent cowgirl. Your heart is so big. You are so courageous that you scare me and you make me admire you, love you for just being you."

His lips landed on hers with more force than he'd intended, but she accepted him, opening to him. He wanted to cherish her and, at the same time, take her right there on the kitchen floor.

When they finally broke the kiss, Payson felt the fragile bond that had been growing between them strengthen. Their new connection gave them each enough room to be themselves, to do what they needed to make themselves happy while supporting each other

She gave him another squeeze, burying her face in his neck, whispering, "Spence was right. They were bluffing. You're not going to Philly. They just said that to scare me."

Payson froze. Philadelphia. How had the hospital known about that? More importantly, what was he going to do? He'd accepted the offer right after the reopening, when he thought nothing was left between him and Jessie. Then they'd been so busy saving Hope's Ride and being together that he hadn't wanted to ruin it. He'd been vacillating about Philadelphia all week, on the brink of calling to tell them that he'd changed his mind.

"What?" Jessie asked.

Payson pulled away slowly feeling the heat of her leave him and the cold dread grow. She'd never understand why he'd made his decision and why he hadn't told her because all of his excuses were stupid, stupid, stupid. He raked his fingers through his hair, trying come up with a way to explain this all to Jessie, to keep her from being hurt and walking away.

"You *are* going there. I can see it on your face." Jessie whirled away. "I was so sure you'd changed. I should have known an Appaloosa can't change his spots." Now, she turned back and the green eyes were bright with anger and the hurt that he dreaded seeing there.

"I said yes before we…" He stumbled to stop.

"Before we what? Before we had sex? Before you used me to—"

"I never used you."

"When were you going to tell me you were leaving? After the moving company showed up?"

"Everything happened so fast. I didn't have a chance to tell you or anyone. Spence doesn't even know. Jessie, I thought—"

"*You* thought it would be best to just run away, to leave all of these children who love Dr. Mac. To leave *me*." A sob escaped from between her tightly sealed lips.

"None of you needed *me*. There are other doctors in the Valley, and you definitely never needed me and certainly don't now. The hospital was clear that there was no promotion for me here. The hospital in Philly called and offered me everything that I had been working for. A chance to try new techniques and make a difference for even more children. It was a chance of a lifetime. I couldn't turn it down, plus we hadn't—"

"How can I compete against that?" Jessie asked quietly. Her shoulders slumped, and her usually confident voice broke as she said, "Go. You need to go now...and not come back."

"But Jessie, I'll tell Philly I changed my mind."

"No. Absolutely not. I don't want you resenting me again."

"I never resented you."

"Payson, we're not reliving our marriage. We're divorced. You're no longer a part of my life, and it needs to stay that way. Go." Her voice had risen and her face whitened.

He wanted to shake her until she understood and took it all back.

"Get out!" she yelled, pushing at him.

He allowed himself to be pushed. "Jessie," he said softly when he stood in the doorway. "You were the reason that I could take care of my patients, that I got through medical school. When you left me, I thought that I'd never help another child."

"Funny," she said with a gasping cry. "When you signed the divorce papers, you said, 'Now, I'll have the time to be a real surgeon.'" Jessie stepped back into the house and closed the door on him.

Payson walked to his Range Rover, not feeling the

ground and not seeing the spectacular Arizona sunset. He could only feel the jagged place in his chest, reliving Jessie telling him that he had to go, that once again he'd come up short and she didn't want him.

Chapter Seventeen

"Molly, stop," Jessie barked. The pony laid back her ears and showed her teeth. "Don't you dare, unless you want to be on hay-only rations for the next week."

Molly stomped her hoof before she slowly went into the stall. The pony didn't press Jessie's patience. Her temper had shortened so much, even Lavonda barely spoke with her. Jessie blamed the stress of Desert Valley dropping the program and Arizona General dragging its feet. Between the two, the future of Hope's Ride remained precarious, despite the fund-raising and the increasing number of youngsters wanting to sign up.

Jessie'd also had calls from people who wanted to study her ranch so they could open similar programs. She hadn't decided exactly how to deal with that and had referred them to the certificate program she'd taken. Right now, about all she could do was get up and paste on her rodeo smile.

Today had started out badly. Molly had helped the other horses escape, which meant lessons started late. The changed routine had made the children whiny and unfocused. Then Spence called and said that Arizona General had put off its decision again. The final cherry on the crappy day had been Alex babbling about Dr.

Mac. She'd barked at him to be quiet, and now her stomach dropped as she remembered how the little boy's face crumpled into tears. How would she ever make it up to him? Let him feed Molly her gummy treats the next time he came out, if he came again?

"Oof." Molly's head smacked Jessie in the middle of the back, making her stumble. She came down hard on her bad knee, which immediately buckled, and she landed in a fresh pile of road apples.

"Damn it!" she shouted. She couldn't stop the tears that streaked down her face as she sat in the stall in a pile of manure that stupidly reminded her of Payson. How pathetic. Road apples. That was what she'd told him so many years ago, what they'd laughed about as she'd told Alex the same story.

Warm, grassy breath blew across her cheek as Molly nuzzled her. She hugged the pony hard and then the usually bad-tempered Bull gently laid his muzzle on her head. Tears leaked from her eyes even with the horsey comfort. She couldn't find that safe place again, where she could care about the children and the program but not think about Payson and not remember when she'd been part of an "us."

Jessie felt as wrung out and limp as a tortilla. She pushed herself to her feet, swaying a little. Had she eaten today? Had anything to drink? Probably. She usually ate with the children and volunteers. No. Today she'd made phone calls over lunch, and she'd gotten up too late for breakfast. That was why she was weepy, low blood sugar. She never cried—well, hardly ever.

Jessie walked out of the stall and double-checked the lock. She limped to the house. Dang. Her jeans were caked with filth. She stood on the back porch and stripped them off. Standing in the near dark in her shirt and panties, she figured that if her life were like one of those movies her sister had watched incessantly when they were teens, then right about now Payson would show up. But he didn't. He wouldn't.

She sighed and went into the quiet house. Before she'd called Payson and he'd come back into her life, she'd liked her house, had even enjoyed the quiet at the end of a long, noisy day. Now, her home echoed. She didn't want to be alone. She wanted to share her life… with Payson.

She turned on every light in the kitchen and then opened the fridge. Getting herself supper would make everything better. Or it might if she actually had any food. She didn't even have a beer. She grabbed the nearly empty jar of salsa and rummaged in the cupboard for an almost-fresh bag of tortilla chips. She brought these to the bedroom, turning on more lights. She sat her dinner on her dresser and dunked a couple of chips in the jar before stripping completely naked so she could head to the shower. She'd been none too fresh before sitting down in the manure. Now, eau de barn clung to her. She'd have a quick shower then watch TV till she fell asleep. The couch doubled as her bed pretty regularly now. *Just do, don't think*, she told herself sternly and headed to the bathroom to clean up.

HAIR DAMP, AND COMFY in a T-shirt and cut-off sweatpants, Jessie sat on the couch with the crumbs in the chip bag and an ice pack on her knee. She'd been standing too many hours even before Molly had pushed her. She'd asked too much of the abused joint, but aspirin and ice took care of most of it.

She aimed the remote control at the TV and flicked through stations. Nothing caught her attention, and she wanted her attention caught. Anything to keep her brain occupied. She couldn't even call Lavonda. Her sister had actually moved from agreeing with every one of Jessie's complaints about Payson to something like cutting the guy a break.

Plus, if Jessie talked with anyone right now, she wouldn't be able to hide how upset she was. Tears hovered, ready to drip down her cheeks if she let her guard down. She'd already cried in the shower. *Think of something else. Find a rodeo to watch.* Except there weren't any rodeos and she didn't care about redecorating her house on a budget. How much longer could she go on like this?

She stared at her phone, not sure if she wanted it to ring and display Payson's number or if she wanted to pick it up and call him. Could she live in Philadelphia? Not that he'd asked her. But Pennsylvania had farmland. It wouldn't be so different. She and Payson could get a place, and they could commute to their jobs—she to a farm and he to the hospital. Was that what she really wanted?

She sat up, staring blindly at the TV. It would mean giving up Hope's Ride, exchanging his dream for hers, for everything she'd worked to save. She sucked in a shaky breath. Was she saying that she wanted Payson, that he was more important than the children? No. She couldn't do that. Her jaw ached with holding back the sobs. This was it. She had to give up on the fantasy of making a relationship with him work or she'd be an even bigger mess.

She lay back on the couch, staring at the ceiling, running through all of the reasons that going forward on her own would be just fine. She'd done it for three years. Darn that little voice that said "fine" hadn't really been all that great. She'd ached at night for Payson and had remembered their happiness at odd times throughout the day. But if she concentrated on the children and Hope's Ride, they would fill every corner of her heart and brain. *Sure*, that nasty inner voice taunted, *but is that enough?* Was it ever enough?

Jessie jumped up, wanting to run away from the voice, from the truth. It was Payson, had always been Payson. Even as she'd built a new life, had she secretly been waiting for him to come back? Was that why she'd started the program? Not because rodeoing was over for her or in memory of their baby, but because it was a connection to him?

She stopped breathing. *The truth, Jessie. Tell yourself the truth.* She loved Payson forever and always.

PAYSON GLANCED AT the clock over the stove when he heard the doorbell ring. Past time for anyone to be visiting him, not that he ever had any visitors. Even Spence never just stopped by. He looked through the narrow window beside the door and felt his heart lurch. Jessie stood on his doorstep, her outline blurry in the light from the lamppost. He yanked open the door.

"What's happened?" he asked, imagining that one of the students needed his help. No other reason could bring her here to him. He hadn't thought he'd see her again. He'd sold his condo and Desert Valley had asked him to leave early. His time in Arizona had dwindled down to days.

Jessie watched him intently. "Can I come in? I need to tell you something."

Deep down, he wanted to take her into his arms and kiss her until she said that she…what? Nothing. She'd made her feelings clear. He had to let her go to find her own happiness without him.

Jessie looked around at the other darkened front doors. She sucked in a deep breath. "I'm sorry. I shouldn't have—"

"Come in here. We don't need to disturb the neighbors," he said, reaching out to take her arm.

She shook off his hand. "No. I'm not ashamed and whoever hears me is fine. I know you're going to Philadelphia and I understand why. I should have let you explain. I should have stayed and talked with you about it. I mean, the Amish have a lot of horses, so it's not so different from here. Well, there aren't Amish in Philadelphia, but they're not far away. I saw that program about them once. Their horses are a little different. You know they buy—"

"Stop," he said. His heart had skipped at least four beats as she spoke. It sounded to him as though she was telling him that she'd move with him. He never would have asked her to give up Hope's Ride for him. "I wish you well and will send a donation to Hope's Ride."

Jessie stepped forward and stuck her foot over the threshold. "You're not sending me away until I say this." Her sage-green eyes glittered. "I don't want you to leave and *I* can't let you go. That means that either I have to fly a whole lot or I need to move to Pennsylvania." She took a deep breath and locked her gaze on him.

"What? You're not making sense. We're divorced and whatever…well, whatever we had is over, too. I'm going to Philly, and you're staying here where a cowgirl belongs."

"Look," she said loudly. "Look down."

He couldn't stop himself from glancing down and he couldn't believe it. His cowgirl had on a pair of horrible green sneakers. "I don't think they wear boots in the East, do they?" she asked, her voice breaking just a little.

"I don't know," he whispered. He tried to wrap his mind around the idea that Jessie would give up Hope's Ride, would give up just about everything to come with him. He didn't resist as she pushed him into his condo. He couldn't think about anything but those damned sneakers. "I think you can see those from space," he said, pointing at her feet as his brain kept working.

Jessie looked down, then smiled up at him. "It was these or pink. You know how I feel about pink. They would probably light my way in the dark, huh?" She turned her foot back and forth to show off the shoe.

He stopped them both toward the living room. "Jessie, you can't come to Philly with me," he said firmly.

"I can do whatever I want."

"I know you can do whatever you want, but I can't let you…sorry, that's not what I mean…it's just that… you're a cowgirl." He didn't know how else to explain it. Jessie belonged here in the desert with her horses, with the scrub, with the heat. She fit.

"You're a surgeon and you belong where you're needed. The children in Philly need you. What is what I want compared to that? Plus, it's not like horses only live in Arizona or that we can only do Hope's Ride here. I've had calls from people all over, wanting to start up similar programs."

He looked again at her bright sneakers, trying to picture Jessie anywhere else. But they were over, done, *terminado*. They had to be because he couldn't take losing her again. "Jessie, you'd never be happy there. I understand that and I can't—"

Jessie moved so fast he didn't have a chance to stop her. She locked her lips on his, kissing him deeply, tenderly, fiercely. He didn't want to respond, but his tongue swept through her mouth, savoring her taste. He groaned in the back of his throat, wrapping his arms around her. How could he leave her? How could he stay? His body didn't care. Her hands kneaded his shoulders and her mouth softened and opened under him. She held nothing back. Even as her vulnerability scared him, her warmth twined around him, fit him like the missing piece of his life that she was. He bruised her mouth with his kiss. This was the last one, he told himself, and then pushed her away.

"No," Jessie said. Her ranch-strong hands grasped his forearm. "I'm not giving up this time. We gave up too easily last time because we didn't understand what we had. I know now how special we are when we're together. I'm not giving up on that. Philadelphia, Hope's Ride—all of that is solvable. What isn't is the hole in my heart when you're not with me. Even when we're fighting, when I'm so mad at you I could do you bodily harm, my heart is whole. These last three years, I didn't know exactly what was wrong. I thought divorcing you would make me feel whole again, would help me get over Violet, that I'd be able to move on. I was wrong."

"You were wrong? Jessie, are you saying that you…" Payson began, and stuttered to a stop.

"I love you," she said with no hint of doubt. "I never stopped loving you."

"Jessie," he choked out. "I can't…how?"

She took both his hands and stood looking at him squarely, her eyes soft. "This is the scariest thing I've ever done, but nothing worthwhile is easy. We know that. I can be brave enough for both of us for right now, until you can—"

He brought her close to him, hugging her so hard that the breath whooshed out of her. "Jessie, Jessie, Jessie." He swallowed hard and choked out. "It's too late. We can't go back."

"That's just stupid," she said, smacking his chest.

"I'm committed to Philadelphia. You're committed to Arizona."

"That's your best argument? It doesn't even make sense. There are planes. I've told you that Hope's Ride is portable."

He let her go and turned away. He turned over what she'd said. His higher-functioning gray matter agreed with her, but that deep-down caveman, living-on-instinct part of his brain yelled at him to run. His gut flipped and he heard Jessie moving. He couldn't let her touch him again. He hurried to the kitchen.

"You're scared," she said, keeping feet of space between them. Her voice was soft and cajoling, like the one she used with a difficult horse.

He laughed, short and hard. "I'm not some bronc you're trying to break."

"You're worse. You're a scared spitless man."

He slammed down the bottle of water he'd pulled from the fridge. "What the hell do you want from me?"

"I want you to be honest with me and yourself."

"You want honesty. I want to love you, but how can I when loving you means you giving up your dream?"

"I already told you how that will work."

"You say it, but there's no way you won't resent me, just like you did when I was a resident, when you lost Violet."

Jessie opened her mouth and then closed it. "I don't have a good track record, but even you can see that I'm different. I came here and I've laid everything on the table. I haven't kept back one thing."

He wanted to believe that they could be different. He didn't want to go to Philadelphia and leave a part of himself here. Was Jessie really telling him the truth not only about her feelings but also about her dreams? "Why now?"

"Even Molly is afraid to cross me," she said, and her smile trembled. "That's not true. Well, it's true, but it's not why. I knew you would be gone and that I'd never see you again. Just the thought of that made me cry. I just sat and cried."

"I...I don't know what to say...what to do."

Jessie hurried to him. "You don't have to do anything but be you. That sounds like a sappy greeting card. But I mean it. I don't want anyone but you." Her green gaze searched his face. "Just like I have to ask for help, you know sometimes you've got to let someone else take the reins."

"You mean you?"

"No. I mean us. Together, honestly, we can do anything. Look what we've already done for Hope's Ride and for all of these children."

He wanted to believe her, and he wanted to believe in what his heart had been telling him. That for him there was no woman but Jessie, never had been and never would be. Could he really drop the reins and let Jessie, fate or whatever take over?

But it wasn't really that, was it? He only needed that control to keep himself from being too scared to do anything, too afraid to make a big mistake. The tightness in his chest loosened. Jessie and he could never be a mistake. Maybe their timing was crappy. They had been too young for marriage, but look at what they had done together now. No matter what, even in the darkest days of their marriage, Payson had known that Jessie would be there for him. Maybe that was what had hurt the most, when she'd turned from him after Violet.

Now, though, the years apart and all of that hurt had taught him so much, including how precious what they had was—and how rare. He looked up. Jessie had moved very, very close and a shiver of awareness raced through him, making him hot and cold at the same time.

"Jessie," he said, his voice low and choked. She closed the millimeters of space between them. His arms automatically went around her, making him feel just right. "My sweet, beautiful cowgirl…I love you," he said with relief. His heart had always known it, but his darned brain had been too afraid to accept the truth. "I love you," he repeated, kissing her mouth, her cheeks, tasting salty tears.

"Payson," she whispered, holding him tightly, her lips closing over his.

He explored her mouth slowly, remembering with joy the pleasure of being together, of loving each other. Her fingertips dug into his shoulders, holding him in place as she darted out her tongue to taste him. Touching her body fed that part of him that had been empty since they'd been apart. He wanted her here and now.

He wanted to take his time, not just steal a few kisses. He ached to show her what she meant to him. How he couldn't and hadn't been really living without her.

"JESSIE, HONEY," PAYSON whispered to her, pulling his lips away enough to speak. "I love you and I want to, you know."

She laughed softly, "Me, too. I want to 'you know' again and again." She scattered small butterfly-soft kisses all over his face, so happy that she couldn't contain the laugh that bubbled out of her. She stood, pulling him with her. She had to kiss him from his toes to his lovely mouth. That very clever mouth that she hoped he'd use to "you know." She laughed again, pulling him to her and kissing him hard.

Payson pulled her more tightly against him with a quick, hard kiss that she turned into a soft meeting of their lips, showing him that she loved him and that she would never leave him again. His hands moved down her body and pushed her away just a little.

"Stop fooling around," she gasped, running her fingers through his thick hair as she tugged him gently toward her to revel in his amazingly expressive and loving mouth.

He moved his head to her touch, but instead of their mouths meeting, his breath whispered across her ear as he said, "Good things come to those who wait." Then his soft lips nibbled their way to the place where her neck met her shoulder. She shuddered delicately. He paused and she made a small noise of protest. He kissed her forehead tenderly. "Not the kitchen tonight. I want you stretched out on my...our bed, where I can see and taste every sweet inch of your skin."

They walked down the hall to his bedroom side by side, hips brushing, fingers entwined. "I'm so glad you kept our bed," she said.

"That should have been a sign, huh?"

"Yes," she said, spinning him to face her, so that he could see into her eyes and could see how serious she was. She kissed him with every ounce of her love. She didn't want him to doubt that this was what she wanted and that he was the only man for her. Her mouth stayed locked on his, her tongue dancing with his, making it clear that she wanted him and what he meant to her. Together she knew now that they could face anything. Her independence did not make her who she was. Loving Payson was what made her the Jessie who could help children, who might just be able to love another child. She clasped him to her.

"I love you, too, Jessie. I will and have always loved you," he said when he broke their kiss just enough to tell her that. It left her with no doubt. He led her to the bed where he slowly, tenderly undressed her. She returned the favor and the two of them renewed their love right there in the bed that had always been the safe and loving place in their marriage.

MUCH LATER, AFTER they'd both lost control and then finally come back to themselves, Payson pressed Jessie's hand to his mouth for a kiss and said, "I know you'll think this is crazy, and I can't believe I'm saying this. I want you to think about us getting married again."

Jessie didn't say anything because her breath had left her. She scrambled to make sense of his words. Finally, she choked out, "That's what I want, too, but—"

"Too soon?"

"No, sweetie, no," she said, squeezing his leg and smiling at him. "But don't you think we need to settle a few things before we consider taking the plunge again?"

He nodded and she saw his face relax into a shy smile. "I'll start. I want to have children."

"I do, too," Jessie said without hesitation.

"I would like us to try right away. When we weren't sure if you were pregnant, I knew then that I wanted children, and I wanted those children with you," Payson said. His dark gaze stayed focused on her and their brightness convinced her that everything he said was coming from his heart. "I know any babies we have won't replace Violet, but having more babies together will honor the love that made her."

The sharp blow of pain she expected didn't come. Talking with him about a future and about babies didn't stir the usual bottomless ache. Instead, she felt tenderness for their baby and for Payson.

"No baby can replace Violet and I want to have a child…children…but I'll definitely need you to be there for everything. The doctor's appointments, the morning sickness, the delivery room, everything."

"Jessie, I promise you now that when we have a baby, I will be so annoying because I want to be a part of everything. You may regret asking me." He stroked her hand.

The last little part of her heart that had been frozen since Violet and the divorce melted. "Then I'll expect you to stick around even when I'm telling you to go and telling you that I can do it all on my own. I need you to remind me that I have to ask for help."

"I promise to remind you. And you'll tell me when

I want to be in control, when I'm trying to orchestrate every detail, right?"

She nodded, leaned forward and kissed him softly with all of the promise of the passion they'd just shared.

"Now, Philadelphia," she said firmly. They talked about their careers and their ambitions. And when they got tired of talking, they snuggled down into the sleigh bed, whispering love to each other until they found sweet oblivion in each other's arms, falling asleep tangled together and content. They knew their love would see them through because they were older, wiser and willing to bend.

"I'm starved," Payson said when they woke after a brief nap. He got up and walked naked to the kitchen. Jessie rolled into the space that smelled like him and their loving. When he came back into the room in all of his yummy nakedness, she didn't even notice the plate in his hand. "Before we eat," he said, "I need you to sit on the edge of the bed."

Then he did the one thing Jessie never expected. Payson knelt before her, taking her hand in his, smoothing his hand over the spot where eventually a ring would go.

"Jezebel Maybelle Leigh MacCormack," he said, keeping his eyes locked with hers. "I love you. I have always loved you and will always love you. I will love the children that we create and I will love the home that we make. Will you marry me?"

"Payson Robert MacCormack, I love you and I will marry you again."

Epilogue

"Oh, hell," said Lavonda, who rarely swore.

Jessie followed her line of sight, sprang out of the rocker and sprinted across the yard. "Molly!" she yelled. The little pony didn't turn. She walked calmly away from the barn with a line of horses following her.

"How can we help?" Lavonda asked as she neared the parade.

Jessie didn't hesitate as she gave Lavonda, Spence and Payson orders about what to do to round up the animals. She would deal with Molly, whose bad behavior had increased exponentially over the past month. Jessie's attention had been diverted by wedding plans that had ratcheted up to full gear and by Payson staying at the house whenever he flew home from Philadelphia. It wasn't a long-term solution, but it worked for now.

Jessie walked toward the little pony with slow steps. Molly backed up and bared her teeth. Calming herself and wishing she had an apple or gummy-worm bribe, Jessie took another step forward.

"She looks like one of my patients when they're being particularly bad," Payson said from behind Jessie's shoulder. Molly stomped her hoof. Jessie felt Payson's stifled chuckle. "What do you want me to do?" he asked softly.

"I want someone to get this pony to behave," she answered. "I'm going to be the worst mother in the world."

Payson had been sure that they'd talked through everything. Parenthood had been at the top of their list. They'd discussed how many children and even which colleges they'd like them to attend. In all of that, Jessie had never said anything about being worried that she couldn't be a good mother. She mothered every single one of the children who came through Hope's Ride. How could she think she wouldn't be good at it? He was the one who had doubts. Sure, he treated young children, but he only worked on their bodies. Anything difficult, like dealing with tears, he usually left to their parents or the nursing staff.

Payson whispered in Jessie's ear, "You will be a great mother. You'll have to help me. I'll be the one who wants everything to run on a schedule and for them to hit every milestone right on time. I'll be the one taking them to the doctor every fifteen minutes. I can't even imagine them as teens."

Jessie made a noise that was somewhere between a sniffle and a laugh. "I keep thinking about being up half the night with the baby and then falling asleep at work and having a child fall off a horse or something. How can I raise children and run Hope's Ride?"

"You'll have help, Jessie," Payson said, and wrapped his arms around her from behind so both of them could keep their eyes on the unpredictable Molly.

"I guess."

"You will, and not just me. Your mom and dad, your siblings, Spence, Helen, everyone will help out. You don't have to do it alone to prove you're the best mother in the world."

"Keep reminding me of that," Jessie said and leaned her head back on his shoulder. He could feel her relaxing. "And I'll remind you that you can't control everything when you try to keep our babies safely locked up in a crib and away from their ponies. I'll remind you of that when they want to borrow the keys to the car."

She was right. They worked together because they understood each other's weaknesses. "I love you, Jessie," he said and let his lips brush against her hair.

She squeezed the arms wrapped around her. "I love you, too, Payson."

They stood for long moments, enjoying the bubble of their love. Everything was right when they remembered that they loved each other.

Jessie was brought back to the dust and heat when she heard a small hoof stamp the ground again, this time followed by a whinny. She didn't move from Payson's arms, but she did glare at Molly.

"What's her problem?" he asked.

"She's annoyed with me."

"For putting her in the barn? I thought she liked staying with Bull. Isn't that why you asked your brother to give you his horse, so she would have her friend?"

"That's not what has her annoyed. I don't even know how a pony can know this, but Lavonda and I were talking about the wedding one day as Molly followed us around. Lavonda said that it would be cute to have Molly as the ring bearer. I said no. Since then she's been acting like a spoiled brat," Jessie said.

"You hurt her feelings?" Payson asked. She could hear something between dismay and humor in his voice.

"Who knows? She might just be miffed because the children aren't paying enough attention to her," Jessie said, exasperated by the pony's behavior.

Jessie hadn't realized that Lavonda and Spence had joined them until her sister spoke. "Jessie's right. Molly has been horrible since she heard she can't be the ring bearer."

"This is exactly why she can't be," Jessie said to the pony.

"Give her a chance, darlin'," Spence drawled.

"Yeah, Jessie, give her a chance," Payson said.

She looked at the pony, who then took a step toward them. Jessie moved reluctantly from Payson's arms and closer to Molly. "All right. You can be the ring bearer, but you only get one piece of cake." The pony nodded her head up and down before sauntering off to the barn.

"Our kids are going to walk all over us," Jessie said to Payson.

"Probably," he said. "But they'll be happy and loved. That's what counts." He pulled her into his arms again and kissed her hard.

JESSIE HAD KNOWN her family wouldn't think anything of Molly acting as ring bearer. Spence hadn't blinked an eye either, but the rest of the MacCormacks, who'd been communicating about the wedding via text and voice-mail, had suggested a number of possible alternatives to an "equine stunt," from a friend of a friend's grandson to simply having no ring bearer. She and Payson had stood firm. Of course, it had all seemed like fun and good times until this minute. Jessie had been called from the house to deal with diva Molly, who'd been laying back her ears and showing her teeth every time anyone got close to her with the pillow. Jessie didn't mind the minicrisis. She'd been at the house going quietly crazy, sitting around in her creamy full-length dress with an overlay of organza and a short train that made her feel feminine and bridal. She'd refused to have any lace, but the softness of the layers kept the dress from being too stark. She and Payson had known that it was unusual to go for a formal wedding the second time, especially when it was to the same person and when it was held in the ranch yard. They wanted to make sure that everyone understood how serious they were about their vows and their commitment to each other.

"Miss Jessie," Alex said as she came over to her. "You look beautiful."

"Thank you, Alex. You look very handsome." She smiled at the little boy in his Western-style tuxedo. He'd been drafted to lead Molly down the aisle.

"Did you give Molly her treat before you tried to put on the pillow?" Jessie asked, addressing both Alex and Lavonda, who was standing nearby in her maid of honor dress—an off-the-rack gown in a ruby red that looked spectacular on her.

"Yep. We also brushed her with her favorite curry comb to get her mane that shiny," Lavonda said. "And we didn't wake her too early." In short, they had followed all of the instructions to keep Molly as happy as possible on this big day.

Jessie admired the pony's shiny coat and the little wreath of flowers sitting jauntily over her ears. "Now, my girl," she said to Molly, "what is your problem? When I told you that you could be the ring bearer, I believe you promised to behave." The pony stomped her hoof in answer, just missing Jessie's white cowgirl-booted foot.

Jessie looked into Molly's brown eyes, trying to understand what had annoyed the pony today of all days. Jessie glanced over and saw Payson pacing at the altar, which had been set up by the catering company that his parents had insisted on hiring. Spence stood near his brother, texting without a pause, even as he smiled vaguely toward a friend of hers.

Jessie looked at Molly again, who now gazed fixedly at Payson. Jessie groaned. Of course the diva was unhappy now that she'd figured out she wouldn't be the center of attention. Well, nothing else about this marriage and ceremony was traditional. There was no reason to think the walk down the aisle would be. She beckoned Payson over.

TEN MINUTES LATER, everyone was ready for the big moment, including Molly. The wedding march started and everyone turned to look down the short aisle, which had been hastily widened so that Payson and Jessie could stand on each side of Molly and the three of them could walk up the aisle. The pony behaved perfectly, lifting her dainty hooves high and arching her neck. Payson looked at Jessie and smiled. She shrugged. Their lives might never be what they had planned, but they loved each other and that was all that mattered.

When they got to the altar, the minister didn't bat an eye at the unusual threesome. By the time he said "You may kiss the bride," Molly had received enough attention that she willingly took a step back. Payson took Jessie into his arms and before he sealed the deal with a kiss, he looked into her sage-green eyes and said, "I love you forever and always, Mrs. MacCormack."

"I love you forever and always, Mr. MacCormack," she replied.

They kissed to the whoops and hollers of those gathered along with a whinny from Molly, which was followed by a chorus of whinnies from the other horses. Before they broke their embrace, Payson whispered, "She is absolutely not going with us on our honeymoon."

* * * * *

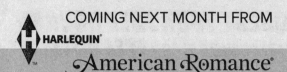

COMING NEXT MONTH FROM

HARLEQUIN®

American Romance®

Available July 7, 2015

#1553 THE COWBOY SEAL'S TRIPLETS
Bridesmaids Creek
by Tina Leonard

John Lopez "Squint" Mathison learned a lot in the Navy, but taming wild child Daisy Donovan requires a different set of skills. Skills he's going to need as an expectant father!

#1554 THE BULL RIDER'S SON
Reckless, Arizona
by Cathy McDavid

When newly hired bull manager and old friend Shane Westcott shows up at the Easy Money Rodeo Arena, Cassidy Beckett is forced to reveal the secret she's been keeping for six years: the identity of her son's father.

#1555 THE HEART OF A COWBOY
Blue Falls, Texas
by Trish Milburn

Natalie Todd has returned to Blue Falls with a terrible secret. She knows she must reveal the truth, but doing so will kill any feelings rancher Garrett Brody has for her...

#1556 A RANCHER OF HER OWN
The Hitching Post Hotel
by Barbara White Daille

Ranch manager and single father Pete Brannigan needs to find the right woman to make his family complete. And Jane Garland is completely unsuitable. So why can't he stop thinking about her?

REQUEST YOUR FREE BOOKS!
2 FREE NOVELS PLUS 2 FREE GIFTS!

HARLEQUIN®

American Romance®

LOVE, HOME & HAPPINESS

YES! Please send me 2 FREE Harlequin® American Romance® novels and my 2 FREE gifts (gifts are worth about $10). After receiving them, if I don't wish to receive any more books, I can return the shipping statement marked "cancel." If I don't cancel, I will receive 4 brand-new novels every month and be billed just $4.74 per book in the U.S. or $5.49 per book in Canada. That's a savings of at least 12% off the cover price! It's quite a bargain! Shipping and handling is just 50¢ per book in the U.S. and 75¢ per book in Canada.* I understand that accepting the 2 free books and gifts places me under no obligation to buy anything. I can always return a shipment and cancel at any time. Even if I never buy another book, the two free books and gifts are mine to keep forever.

154/354 HDN GHZZ

Name _____ (PLEASE PRINT) _____

Address _____ Apt. # _____

City _____ State/Prov. _____ Zip/Postal Code _____

Signature (if under 18, a parent or guardian must sign)

Mail to the **Reader Service**:
IN U.S.A.: P.O. Box 1867, Buffalo, NY 14240-1867
IN CANADA: P.O. Box 609, Fort Erie, Ontario L2A 5X3

Want to try two free books from another line?
Call 1-800-873-8635 or visit www.ReaderService.com.

* Terms and prices subject to change without notice. Prices do not include applicable taxes. Sales tax applicable in N.Y. Canadian residents will be charged applicable taxes. Offer not valid in Quebec. This offer is limited to one order per household. Not valid for current subscribers to Harlequin American Romance books. All orders subject to credit approval. Credit or debit balances in a customer's account(s) may be offset by any other outstanding balance owed by or to the customer. Please allow 4 to 6 weeks for delivery. Offer available while quantities last.

Your Privacy—The Reader Service is committed to protecting your privacy. Our Privacy Policy is available online at www.ReaderService.com or upon request from the Reader Service.

We make a portion of our mailing list available to reputable third parties that offer products we believe may interest you. If you prefer that we not exchange your name with third parties, or if you wish to clarify or modify your communication preferences, please visit us at www.ReaderService.com/consumerchoice or write to us at Reader Service Preference Service, P.O. Box 9062, Buffalo, NY 14240-9062. Include your complete name and address.

HARI5

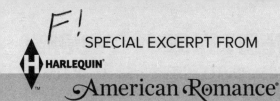
Jane's gaze was steady on her. "John left town last night."

Daisy blinked. "Left town?"

The older woman hesitated, then sat across from her. Cosette Lafleur—Madame Matchmaker herself—slid in next to Jane, her pink-frosted hair accentuating her all-knowing eyes.

Daisy's heart sank. "He *couldn't* have left." He hadn't said goodbye, hadn't even mentioned he was planning to make like a stiff breeze and blow away.

The women stared at her with interest.

"Did you want him to stay, Daisy?" Jane asked.

"Well—" Daisy began, not knowing how to say that she'd thought she at least rated a "goodbye," considering she'd gotten quite in the habit of enjoying a nocturnal meeting in his arms. "It would have been nice."

"Have you finally realized where your heart belongs, Daisy?" Cosette asked, and Daisy started.

"My heart?" How was it that these women always seemed to read everyone's mind? A girl had to be very careful to keep her secrets tight to her chest. "Squint and I are friends."

Cosette winked at her, and a spark of hope lit inside her that maybe Cosette wasn't horribly angry or holding a grudge with her about the whole taking-over-her-shop thing.

"We know all about those kinds of friends," Cosette said, nodding wisely.

"Still," Jane said, "it does seem rather heartless of John to leave without telling you. Had you quarreled?"

Here it came, the well-meaning BC interference of which many suffered, all secretly cherished and she'd never had the benefit of experiencing. She had to say it was rather like being under a probing yet somehow friendly microscope. "We didn't quarrel."

"But you're in love with him," Cosette said.

"That may be putting it a bit—" Her words trailed off.

"Mildly?" Jane asked.

"Lightly?" Cosette said. "You are in fact head over heels in love with him?"

Daisy felt herself blush under all the scrutiny. Sheriff Dennis McAdams slid into the booth next to her, and the ladies wasted no time filling in the sheriff, who turned his curious gaze to her.

"He left last night," the sheriff said, and Daisy wondered if John Lopez Mathison had stopped by to see every single denizen of this town to say goodbye—except for her.

Don't miss THE COWBOY SEAL'S TRIPLETS
by Tina Leonard, available July 2015
wherever Harlequin® American Romance®
books and ebooks are sold.

www.Harlequin.com

HARLEQUIN®

A *Romance* FOR EVERY MOOD™

Love the Harlequin book you just read?

Your opinion matters.

Review this book on your favorite book site, review site, blog or your own social media properties and share your opinion with other readers!

Be sure to connect with us at:
Harlequin.com/Newsletters
Facebook.com/HarlequinBooks
Twitter.com/HarlequinBooks

JUST CAN'T GET ENOUGH?

Join our social communities
and talk to us online.

You will have access to the latest
news on upcoming titles and special
promotions, but most importantly,
you can talk to other fans about your
favorite Harlequin reads.

Harlequin.com/Community

Facebook.com/HarlequinBooks

Twitter.com/HarlequinBooks

Pinterest.com/HarlequinBooks

HARLEQUIN®

A *Romance* FOR EVERY MOOD™

**Stay up-to-date on all your
romance-reading news with the
Harlequin Shopping Guide,
featuring bestselling authors, exciting new
miniseries, books to watch and more!**

The newest issue will be delivered right to you
with our compliments! There are 4 each year.

Signing up is easy.

EMAIL

ShoppingGuide@Harlequin.ca

WRITE TO US

HARLEQUIN BOOKS
Attention: Customer Service Department
P.O. Box 9057, Buffalo, NY 14269-9057

OR PHONE

1-800-873-8635 in the United States
1-888-343-9777 in Canada

Please allow 4-6 weeks for delivery of the first issue by mail.

THE WORLD IS BETTER WITH

Romance

Harlequin has everything from contemporary, passionate and heartwarming to suspenseful and inspirational stories.

Whatever your mood, we have a romance just for you!